MW01134209

WINTER'S
PROMISE

THE BLUE SIDED HUMAN WILL CHOOSE A SIDE.
WHEN FOUR PRINCES ARE BORN ON THE SAME DAY, THEY WILL RULE TRUE.
HER SAVIOUR WILL DIE WHEN THE CHOICE IS MADE.
IF SHE CHOOSES WRONG, SHE WILL FALL.
IF SHE CHOOSES RIGHT, THEN SHE WILL RULE.
ONLY HER MATES CAN STOP HER FROM THE DESTRUCTION OF ALL.
IF THE FATES ALLOW, NO ONE NEED FALL.
FOR ONLY THE TRUE KINGS HOLD HER FATE, AND THEY WILL BE HER MATES.

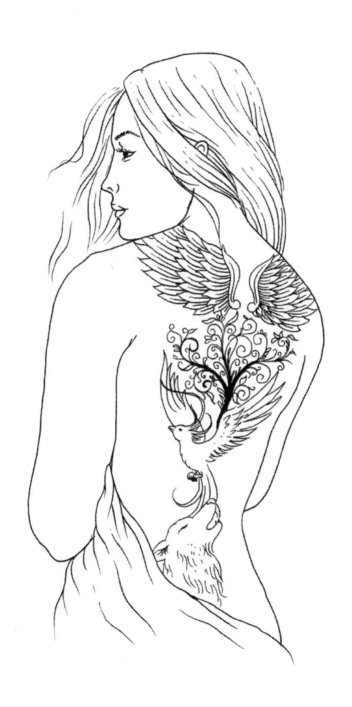

WINTER'S PROMISE

HER GUARDIANS SERIES

WINTER'S PROMISE

HER GUARDIANS SERIES BOOK THREE

G. BAILEY

MORE BOOKS BY G. BAILEY

HER GUARDIANS SERIES

HER FATE SERIES

PROTECTED BY DRAGONS SERIES

LOST TIME ACADEMY SERIES

THE DEMON ACADEMY SERIES

DARK ANGEL ACADEMY SERIES

SHADOWBORN ACADEMY SERIES

DARK FAE PARANORMAL PRISON SERIES

SAVED BY PIRATES SERIES

THE MARKED SERIES

HOLLY OAK ACADEMY SERIES

THE ALPHA BROTHERS SERIES

A DEMON'S FALL SERIES

THE FAMILIAR EMPIRE SERIES

FROM THE STARS SERIES

THE FOREST PACK SERIES

THE SECRET GODS PRISON SERIES

THE REJECTED MATE SERIES

FALL MOUNTAIN SHIFTERS SERIES

ROYAL REAPERS ACADEMY SERIES

THE EVERLASTING CURSE SERIES

COPYRIGHT

For my lovely Nan, Jacqueline. Thank you for always supporting me.

DESCRIPTION

War is coming.
The prophecy is coming true.
When the world is close to falling, and all those she loves are in danger, what can Winter do to save everyone?
Winter finally has the answers to who she is, but everything else in her life is in question.
How much of her past can control her future?
Can Winter make the decisions she needs to save the future?
Follow Winter in the third instalment in Her Guardians series.
Reverse Harem Series

CHAPTER 1

"*Winter knows, Winter knows,*" the childlike voice sings around the frozen field, and as usual, I can't find the singer, but Elissa is here. I can feel her next to me before I even turn to look at her.

"I have a lot of questions," I say, as I look around the cold world we are standing in. The song plays over and over in the background, stuck like an old record.

Elissa is standing completely still as the cold wind whips around her, as if she isn't really here. I want to reach out and shake her, but I can't. Elissa's long black hair flies in the cold wind, mixing with her swaying white dress. Her blue eyes watch me closely, not saying a word.

"I'm related to you, aren't I?" I ask when she doesn't respond to me. I don't need her answer because I'm sure I already know. I just don't want to know.

"You are my only granddaughter," she says.

It's all real, what the demon king said about me, and it makes me feel like my world is crashing down. My mother lied to me; she can't be my mother when this woman's daughter must be.

"The demon king wasn't lying," I say.

Pain haunts her face as she speaks. "Every word he says is usually a lie but not this time. I loved him and had a child with him many years ago," she says the words slowly. Her eyes are glazed with unshed tears. I want to comfort her, but I can't. I don't really know her; she is still a stranger to me.

"My mother?" I ask, and she nods.

"She was half demon and half goddess. You have a lot of her in you, but what's important is the human side you got from your father," she says and moves closer. I hold my breath as she goes to rest a hand on my shoulder but changes her mind at the last second.

"Why is it important?" I ask her.

"Every little thing is important in the end," she whispers and steps back.

"Riddles again," I mutter, trying to move forward, but it's no use. The cold wind gets stronger and blows into my face as I hear her speak.

"You call my spirit into your dreams, but I cannot tell you everything. Look into the past, and you will find the future."

"That makes no sense, Elissa. None of this does, every-thing is going wrong! The demons are taking over, and he is back!" I shout. I have to hold my hands in front of my face, as the wind gets stronger. I can't see Elissa anymore.

"It's not too late. The past, Winter, find the past!" she shouts at me over the wind, and everything goes blurry as I feel myself falling.

"Win, babe, wake up," Alex's voice comes through the haze as I open my eyes. The bed is empty where I'm sleeping, Jaxson no longer in it. His shirt is stuck to me with sweat, and my hair is all over my face. I push it out of the way as I sit up.

Alex looks stunning as usual; her red hair is up high in a ponytail, and her makeup is done to perfection. Not that she needs it.

"Where's Jax?" I ask her, rubbing my eyes. I glance at the clock on Jaxson's bedside table; it says it's only seven in the morning. What happened to sleeping in?

"Jax is with Dabriel and Atti. Wyatt is helping Jax's aunt with the last of the funeral arrange-ments," she says.

"It's today," I mumble, suddenly remembering

we are burying Atti's mother today. The days are mixing together with my guilt over letting the demon king free and my worrying about how we are going to survive this. Atti is distant with me; well, he won't even speak to me. Jaxson says it's just his way of coping, and it isn't anything to do with me. I don't believe that.

"Has Atti spoken to you yet?" Alex asks.

"No, he won't let me close, I'm worried he's going to do something stupid like go straight to the dark witch queen and try to kill her," I say, watching as Alex looks at me closely.

"Why would that be bad? That bitch totally needs a kick up the ass," Alex says, and I just notice that she's dressed in all white. I'm really not with it, that dream with Elissa is stuck in my mind. What did she mean about my past?

I know I need to speak to my mum, but how can I just ask her? How can I even look at her without feeling so angry that she has lied to me? I'm sure she had a reason, but doesn't everyone deserve to know who their parents are?

I eye the white dress on the end of the bed.

"Not black?" I ask.

"No, light witches wear white to their funerals. Drake said it's a tradition of theirs. Atti can't bury his mother where she deserves, so the funeral needs to be as close as it can to a witch's funeral," she explains.

"Oh right, I guess that makes a lot of sense," I say quietly.

"I still think he should go and kill the queen."

"It would be a bad idea. He can't just kill the new queen. Not only has she been messing with the demons, but she is also going to be very powerful. The people respect her, she won the crown. Atti could kill her, but he wouldn't win the people that way. Atti is a light witch, the dark witches will not follow him, and the city would be at war."

"I still think Atti could take her," Alex huffs. I know how she feels; I want to kill the stupid queen for hurting Atti that way.

"You haven't met her," I say with a small smile.

"I'm just saying that guy is built like a tank," she says and winks at me.

"I haven't noticed," I mumble.

"Don't go holding back on me now. How is werewolf sex?" she asks.

I go bright red murmuring, "Err."

"Does he prefer doggy style?" she asks, making me laugh. I go to tell her to mind her own business when the door is slammed open.

"Milo ate all the good food in the house," Freddy says as he comes in the room. Milo, my own little sub-demon, comes flying in behind him and lands on my lap. Alex bought some doll clothes for him, so he doesn't have to wear those rags we found him in. Now, he looks a little like a sailor, with white shorts and a blue shirt with an anchor in the middle. He has his blue hair tied with a little, blue headband. Overall, he looks like a little Smurf, a really cute one with light-silver wings.

"Milo, not the chocolate," I say, and he nods; the melted chocolate all over his face is a good giveaway.

"He ate it all, Winter, and every bit of junk food he could find. Uncle J is going to go ape when he sees his chocolate brownies are gone," Freddy says in annoyance. I smile over at him, seeing he is dressed in white trousers and a crinkle-free, white shirt. I slide out of bed and put Milo on the dresser.

"Freddy, your tie is a little crooked, come here," I wave him over, and he lets me straighten it up before I kiss the top of his head as he hugs me. Wyatt chooses that moment to walk into the bedroom, seeing me hugging his son. Wyatt and Freddy haven't said two words to each other since

Jaxson introduced them. Freddy just said he didn't like vampires and stormed off. Wyatt is just as stubborn and won't talk about it. They are way too similar. I don't think Wyatt has any plans to tell Freddy who he is anytime soon. It wasn't a good father and son meeting. It doesn't help that Freddy has no idea who Wyatt is to him. Or the fact he is half vampire, half wolf in the first place.

I guess Wyatt has a lot of problems at the moment to deal with, like the fact no one can get near the vampire castle. There's a massive red barrier that's appeared around it. Jaxson sent wolves out to find any survivors, and Wyatt went with them a week ago. That's when he saw the barrier. We haven't been able to find anyone. Not a single human or vampire that had escaped.

"I'm happy you're here, can we watch Harry Potter again? You're the only one that likes it," Freddy says.

"Didn't you watch it with Dabriel last night?" I ask.

"Yes, but he kept pausing the first film to ask me questions. I'm not watching anymore with him," he says.

"Hi, Wyatt," I say, and Freddy turns around quickly. Wyatt has a white shirt on, and it's tucked into smart white trousers. His blonde hair has been cut since I saw him yesterday, and now it's just an inch short all over his head. It's styled to the left away from his eyes–eyes that are watching me. A feeling of warmth and love flows over me from him through our bond. I can tell it's him because of how it feels; it's different from my own emotions.

"When are you leaving, vampire?" Freddy asks tensely, a slight growl coming out with his words. Freddy may not know who he is, but Wyatt gets a response out of him every time they're in the same room. Jaxson thinks it Freddy's wolf that's sensing who Wyatt is, but Freddy won't listen. He's too young to truly understand.

"That's not nice," I tell Freddy, but he doesn't respond as he stares down Wyatt. His skin is shaking, and I'm sure he's close to shifting.

"My name is Wyatt, and I am the prince of the vampires. I will not be leaving, and you would do wise to learn some respect," Wyatt says.

Oh god, he's going all dad-mode already. It's really bad that I think it's hot.

"Whatever," Freddy says and storms out of the room, slamming the door shut and making the whole wall shake.

"He is already acting like a teenager! Holy

smokes, you two will have your hands full," Alex comments, and we both glare at her. She holds her hands up in surrender.

"I'll take Milo for a bath," she says and picks him up. He smiles at me with a cheeky grin and tries to move closer to Alex as she holds him with one hand.

"Don't try to hug me, I'm wearing white, you little demon," she says, and I hear Milo laughing as they walk out. Wyatt closes the door and turns to face me.

"How's Atti?" I ask him.

"He needs you, but he doesn't know how to talk to you," he tells me as he moves to stand close to me. He smooths a hand down my hip and watches me. Every touch with Wyatt feels like pleasure, even when Jaxson's shirt is in the way.

"Oh," I say a little breathless.

"Winter," Wyatt says, and he turns away from me. I place my hand on his back as he stares up at Jaxson's sword on the wall.

"I called myself a prince, but I'm not really anymore. My people are likely all dead or demons by now," he says quietly.

"You couldn't save them," I say. There was nothing we could have done, and it's not Wyatt's fault. It's mine; it was my blood that opened that hellhole in the first place.

"Isn't that what a king is meant to do?" he asks.

"What? Die for no reason?" I move around him, glancing up at his glowing, dark eyes, and watching as his teeth grow in anger. I feel my teeth respond without my control. I'm sure my eyes are glowing silver now.

"Yes, kings die for their people. I ran like a coward," Wyatt says, his power slipping into his words and making my head hurt.

"You didn't have a choice, you had no weapons and were weakened. If you stayed, I would have died." I know the words are true. I grab his head and try to turn him to look at me, but he just stares at the sword.

"We would both be dead or worse," I tell him angrily. My hands start glowing blue as I hold them around his face, and he finally looks down at me.

"I failed them, my people. How do you know I won't fail you?" he asks me. Every word is filled with desperation. I know his worst fear is to lose me; I don't need to feel the fear through our bond to know that. Wyatt looks at the ground, like he can't hear my answer.

"Because I believe in you," I tell him, lifting his

head with my hands. I press my lips gently to his, and he kisses me back. I feel his relief and strength in our bond; it's enough to make me know I've gotten through to him. Being around Freddy is so much more difficult than he can tell me. Wyatt told me one day that he looks so much like Demi. I break away from the kiss when Wyatt's hands start raising Jaxson's shirt, knowing this can't go any further right now.

"I'm going to get dressed," I tell him, and he nods with a little smirk. I glance over my shoulder as I grab the dress and some new underwear, then go into Jaxson's bathroom. Wyatt is standing where I left him, a predatory look in his eyes, a look full of promise for our future.

CHAPTER 2

"*I* like you in white," Wyatt says, once I come out of the bathroom fully clothed in the long, white dress. It reminds me of the dress I wear in my dreams, but Alex wouldn't have known that when she brought it to me. I left my long, brown hair down, and it circles around my arms as it stops at my waist. It's perfectly straight and frizz free, someone needs to learn how to sell this vampire hair shit. They would make a fortune.

We both walk out of Jaxson's room and through the house. Lucinda, Jaxson, and Freddy are in the kitchen when we walk in.

"Lovely as always, lass," Jaxson says and stops cutting up sandwiches to come over to me. He kisses me gently then moves away.

"Blood sucker," Freddy mutters and goes back to playing with his phone. I hold in a chuckle when Wyatt glares at him.

"That's very rude, young laddie. It's like calling us a dog, we don't like that," Lucinda tells him off and takes his phone from him.

"Give it back," he says.

"No. Prince Wyatt, here you go. When my nephew decides to be nice, you may give it back," Lucinda says, and Wyatt takes the phone. He holds it up with a smirk and slides it into his shirt pocket.

"So unfair," Freddy complains.

I give him a warning look as he looks at me. I'm not helping him, no matter how cute he is. "Where's Atti?" I ask while stealing one of the sandwiches Jaxson is cutting up. Jaxson laughs as I quickly move out of the way when he tries to take the sandwich I took back. A girl has to eat. I move next to Wyatt as he stands the near the door.

"With Dabriel, Freddy can take you to them," Jaxson replies, and Freddy jumps up.

"Let's go, Winter," Freddy says and grins at me. Waving goodbye to everyone, Freddy and I head outside.

I follow Freddy past the training cabin, which looks full of wolves fighting in both their human and wolf forms. It's interesting to see. We pass several wolves, all of them bowing to me, and I have to remember they see me as their queen now. All of them are in white, and some are tying white ribbons around the trees.

"Is that Leigha and Harris fighting?" I ask Freddy, when we come around the other side of one the cabins. There are several wolves watching as Harris and Leigha fight with swords. They're both good as they circle each other and keep coming back for blow after blow. Harris knocks Leigha's legs out from under her and somehow gets her on her back with him kneeling over her. His sword is pressed against hers over her neck.

I never thought I'd see anyone beat the warrior princess. Neither moves as they stare each other down.

"They've been fighting every day; I think he likes the vampire. Gross," Freddy says.

"You do realise I'm part vampire, right?" I ask Freddy. Harris helps Leigha up, and they both talk quietly as the wolves who were watching walk away.

"Yeah, but you're different."

"No, I'm not. Wyatt isn't that bad, and I love him, Freddy. I know you don't trust him, but do you trust me?" I ask, and he watches me carefully with his bright brown eyes.

"Yes."

"Then give him a break. Not everything is as it seems," I say, and he hugs me. I press a kiss on his forehead.

"Come on, they don't seem to have noticed that we're here," I say as he lets go. I watch as Harris lays a hand on Leigha's arm, and she blushes. Actually blushes. Holy crap, the warrior princess has a crush on a wolf. I have to admit that Harris is hot. He has that sexy, wavy, blond hair and massive build you expect to see on a surfer. I know he did well with girls at the university we went to. The girls would all talk about the hot guy that sometimes came to parties. Even Alex had her eye on Harris before she met Drake.

Freddy walks us through the woods until we see Dabriel and Atti in a clearing.

Dabriel is talking quietly to Atti, who is on his knees in front of a white casket. It's decorated beautifully in lots of white flowers and little lights. Dabriel places his hand on Atti's shoulder, and they both stare at the coffin. My heart breaks for Atti.

"Freddy, go back, and thanks for bringing me," I say.

"Sure," he says and hugs me before running off.

I walk over, and Dabriel lifts his head as I get closer. Atti goes tense, but he doesn't face me. They're both dressed in white. Dabriel's large wings are resting close to his back. Now that I'm so near, I can see the slits in the back of his shirt that make room for them. Dabriel's unusually bright purple eyes watch me; sadness is written all over him. "Winter."

I rest my hand on his arm as I get close. "Can I speak with Atti alone?" I ask. I glance down at Atti, his hair is a mess, and he has a beard now. The effect suits him; his clothes are in better condition than how I've seen him in the last two weeks. Atti has been drinking himself silly and passing out. The guys have taken turns watching him. I tried at the start to be there for him, but he just disappeared on me every time I got close. I don't think he could stand me being near him. It wasn't my fault his mother died, but if he wasn't looking after me, he could have saved his mum. At least, that's what I think.

"Okay, Winter," Dabriel says and steps away after kissing my forehead. I watch as he spreads his large, white wings and flies away. I've never seen him fly before; it's pretty cool. I wait until he's just a white line in the trees before I look back at Atti who's gripping his knee fiercely.

I go to my knees next to Atti and slide my hand over the one on his knee. "Atti," I say gently.

When he finally turns to look at me, his face is filled with pain and grief. I place my other hand on his cheek, and he leans into it. We don't talk as we stare at each other like this, I want to be there for him in any way I can.

"*The last time I spoke to her, she told me to be with you. I think she knew her death was coming,*" Atti says gently into my mind. I wish I could talk back into his mind so I don't have to break the strange silence that has happened between us.

"Tell me about her," I whisper as quietly as I can.

"My mother was strong. So strong. She told me once that she slapped my father when they first spoke. He was a rude king, and she didn't want anything to do with him. The rest of the women at the court would do anything for him, but she wouldn't. She told me that my dad said he fell in love with her the moment she slapped him," he says out loud, his voice still quiet. I chuckle, and he continues, "My mother said they were so happy when I was born. The castle shook that day, and when it stopped, the castle was full of flowers. They were everywhere, and every witch said the castle glowed like a rainbow. The war was still happening, and my mother won it. But it was at the cost of her mate, my dad. Most people would have given up, but she didn't. Oh no, she won her throne in the arena and brought me up. She was a great mum, even with her responsibility to the city."

"She sounds like a strong woman."

"The strongest I've ever known. Sometimes acting normal is the hardest thing to do, and she did it well. I always knew she was sad."

"I am sorry, Atti."

"I know," he whispers and pulls me onto his knee. I rest my head on his shoulder and wrap my arms around him as he holds me.

We don't move for a long time. He's silent, and I just don't know what to say anymore.

I watch as Jaxson, Dabriel, and Wyatt walk over to us from the trees. They stand behind us, and I see Alex, Drake, Leigha, and Freddy standing near as they come over. The rest of the wolves stand in the trees, holding little white lanterns and bowing their heads. They're bowing for a queen they didn't know, a queen that wasn't even theirs. It's a sign that one day we can work together, all of us.

"It's time," Atti says. I get up, and offer him my hand to help him up. He accepts and kisses my cheek before he moves away from me. Atti walks up slowly and places his hand on the wooden coffin. The coffin is wrapped in white cloth, and flowers are spread all around. The top of the coffin is a crown made out of wood. I have a feeling Jaxson made it for Atti.

"May the true light guide your way. May you find your home. And may you always know peace," Atti says the words slowly, every word filled with pain and hope.

He steps back and raises both his hands. The coffin bursts into a slow fire that turns white as we watch, and little white lights fly out of it into the sky. We all watch as they fill the sky. The wolves start howling quietly, the noise filling the sad day.

I move forward and hold Atti's hand as silent tears run down his face.

"Goodbye, my strong mother, I will avenge you," Atti's voice whispers in my mind. The resounding howls tell me he told everyone that thought.

I hope the dark witch queen heard it, too.

CHAPTER 3

I run my fingers over Atti's cheek as I'm lying on top of him on the sofa, and he's fast asleep. I slide off him and cover him with a spare blanket. He grumbles a little, but I think he hasn't slept in a while. He stayed quiet after the funeral, wanting to just watch movies, and we all just stayed with him. I told the guys to go to bed after the film, and they did. I walk out of the lounge and through the kitchen to the back door. I open it quietly and nod at the wolf sitting outside. The wolf nods its head, and I walk past.

I open the training room door and flick the light on.

The training room looks different these days. There are more weapons around because of all the training going on and the sheer number of wolves they have here.Every day, Jaxson has to deal with fights over the female wolves, guys thinking they are the stronger wolf, or simple arguments because they don't like each other. It's not easy to have so many wolves in one place. His aunt Lucinda and her mates help with a lot of the problems, so Jaxson can focus on training the pack. I smile as fond memories of my time with Jaxson come rushing back as I look over the room. There on the floor is the first place he kissed me, even if he was a dick afterwards. I run my hand over the crossbow on the wall, and think how things were different before.

"You should never run from a wolf. I will always find you," a deep voice says behind me. I glance over, seeing Jaxson standing with his arms crossed at the door to the training room. He has no shirt on, showing off the impressive chest from all the training. His jeans are hanging low on his hips, and I bet he hasn't got any boxers on.

"I wasn't running," I say with red cheeks and turn fully to face Jaxson. He smiles as he walks over to me.

"A shame, I like to chase you," he says.

"You always catch me in the end," I whisper as he smirks.

"Yes, I always will, lass," Jaxson says and slides his hand into my hair. I let him pull my head to his and press his slightly warm lips to mine. I run my hand up his chest, loving being so close to him.

"How are you?" he asks when we both break away. I stay in his arms as we talk.

"I'm fine," I say.

He looks at me. "I'm calling bullshit on that, lass." I shrug, and he continues, "I know you've been focused on Atti, but you just found out about your true family."

"I'll be better when I find the strength to talk to my mum about this all," I say.

"There's no rush, I have ten wolves watching her constantly, and Dabriel has a light angel watching her, too. She's safe for now. If anything happens, we'll bring her here and explain everything," he tells me.

"She's not my biological mother. I doubt I have any relation to her at all. My mother was a half goddess and half demon. What the hell does that make me?" I say, hating every word, but it's all true. She can't be. The demon king's last words to me are running through my mind. Did he kill my real mother? His daughter? It makes no sense.

"I know," Jaxson replies.

"I'm quarter goddess, quarter demon, and what human side I had, is now vampire," I say. I'm sure he came to the same conclusion as I did.

He nods, "I agree, the human half of you was turned, but the rest of you couldn't, because it's too strong."

I'm half vampire in a way, but I'm more than that. I guess I have always been strange. I never got sick as a child. Not even a cold. That should have told me that something was up. It's funny how you make excuses about weird shit in your life until you have to face the problem. I think I've always done it. My mother doesn't like the winter months, but she named her daughter after them? The dreams; I should have guessed from those alone. "I'm complicated," I mumble, and Jaxson laughs.

"That sums you up, lass," he smirks down at me. "Harris and his mother wish to speak to you as soon as possible. I'm not sure what it's about, but she is a good woman.

"It's about some books on the goddess. Katy told me her mother knows some things."

"Anything we can learn could help us," Jaxson says.

"Can we go and see my mother tomorrow? Atti

might take us, or we'll drive," I say. I know I have to get this over with.

"I'll take you," Atti says, stepping out of the shadows of the doorway and walking over to us.

"You alright, man?" Jaxson asks. Atti shakes his head, his eyes never leaving mine.

"I'll take you to your mother, and then we'll make a plan to take my throne back," he says. The challenge is clear in his eyes; he wants to know if I'm on his side.

"I'm at your side, always," I say, and he nods sternly before he disappears. "Atti has changed," I mumble as I watch the doorway where he once was.

"Don't think too much on his grief. I can understand it, and he will be okay in time," Jaxson says, reminding me that his mother and father are dead, too. That he also lost his sister and brother. When will the men I love stop losing people? "You need to feed," Jaxson says. I guess he's right, I haven't fed in a week, and my teeth keep coming out. Normal food starts tasting bland after a while.

"Yes," I say, watching his neck, and he pulls me close to him. I don't refuse his offer when he turns his head to the side. I bite into his neck, and he holds me close as he groans.

"Winter," he says, and I feel him pull my dress

up as I hold his neck close. My underwear is ripped away, and his jeans fall to his feet just before he slides inside me. I let go of his neck to kiss him, and he kisses me back as he pounds into me.

"I've always wanted to have you in this room," Jaxson says gruffly, and I smile for a second as he lays me down on the cold floor and shows me everything he ever wanted to do to me in this room.

CHAPTER 4

*A*tti holds me close as we appear outside my mother's house, my old home. All day I've been fretting about coming here. About seeing her. Alex finally told me I needed to do this, and I asked Atti to bring me.

I only want Atti with me, and the others seem to understand that. I didn't think about how this might hurt him, seeing my mother when he just lost his, but he didn't refuse. I breathe in his flower-like scent for a second before turning in his tight arms to look at the house on the empty street. I first spot the car parked in front; it's not one I recognise. The two wolves sitting in it, I do.

"*That is not inconspicuous*," Atti whispers in my

mind, as he must be thinking the same thing as I am.

The three=bedroom beach house looms over me as I finally look at it. Everything looks the same about the house I grew up in, the same white, painted, wooden decking surrounding the house. The same blue-panel, wooden walls look like my mum has painted them recently. The grey slate roof and the small, green garden at the front of the house look just like they did when I was a child. The back of the house has a large decking that leads onto a long path towards the beach. The beach is a little rocky, but it's nice to watch the ocean from.

Everything about this house is as homcy as my mum. Yet it feels like a lie, and I feel like a stranger as I stand outside. I remember pulling my suitcase out to my car with my mum and Alex at my side. We both hugged mum goodbye and left with tear-filled eyes. She cried the day we moved out, she cried at every one of my plays at school. My mother does care about me, I know that, but I can't help the anger I feel.

A flash of light from the bright sun hits a car as it drives by. It's a nice day; the sea air fills my senses.

"I'm glad the whole vampire and sunlight thing

is a fake rumour," I tell Atti, and he smiles.

"I think the garlic rumour is the worst one. I once filled Wyatt's bedroom with garlic as a joke. He chased my ass around for a month after that. He got me back when he cut my hair off when I passed out drunk with the guys one night," he says with a slight smile.

"Did you have long hair then?" I ask.

"Yes, it used to be as long as D's. I was growing it out when I met you but—" he stops as I look at him, his grey eyes swirling like an oncoming storm. I've never seen his eyes like this; it's a reminder of how powerful he is.

"But what?" I ask as he stares down at me.

"Winter?" My mum's voice comes from the house stopping Atti's reply. I see her drop her bag and run to me, leaving the front door open. My mum has aged well, and she doesn't have a wrinkle on her face like most women her age. Her blonde hair is cut short in a bob; she has little grey for her fifty-year old self. My mum has on three-quarter length jeans and a white top. She pulls me into a hug the minute she can. Her homey smell hits me, it's like I can smell the home-cooked food and sweet perfume she has always worn. I hold her closer; I need this second of normalcy.

"You look different," she says as she pulls back.

"Not that much," I laugh, and she looks at me closely, too closely. I forgot about the changes in my appearance. At a distance, I look the same, but my mum is too close. She knows my hair wouldn't behave this well, or my eyes don't shine so brightly. I best make sure she doesn't see my marks; she'd have a heart attack thinking they were tattoos. I remember when Alex got one done by her short-term boyfriend when she was sixteen. It's an infinity symbol on her hip. It wasn't a bad tattoo, luckily, considering she let her boyfriend choose it. Mum went crazy when she saw it; Alex was grounded for two months and had a list of stuff to clean every weekend.

"Who's your friend?" Mum says, looking at Atti and snapping me out of the thoughts of the past. I can't be lost in them anymore.

"I'm Atticus Lynx, the boyfriend," Atti introduces himself, and I realise I didn't know his last name. In fact, I only know Wyatt's last name. I make a mental note to ask them all later.

"A boyfriend? You didn't tell me about this handsome one," my mom scolds me.

"There have been a lot of changes that we need to talk about, mum," I say. We both stare at each other, me watching her dark-blue eyes, and eventually she nods.

"You best come in then," she says and walks in the house. Atti links his hand with mine as we follow.

The inside of the house is a large open-plan kitchen to the left and the lounge has big French doors, so you can see the sea. There's a white, modern fireplace with a white sofa in front of it. Two white armchairs are next to the sofa, and there's a white dresser with a mirror by the start of the corridor to the upstairs three bedrooms.

"Would you like some tea?" she asks us.

"No thanks, mum," I answer.

"Two sugars, no milk. Thanks, Winter's mum," Atti says, and I smile.

"Oh, call me Daniella," she waves a hand at Atti who nods. I sit on the sofa with Atti while mum makes tea. She comes in and gives him his then sits in the armchair with her own.

"What brings you home?" she asks. It's best to get straight to the point, I'm too angry not to. I'm twenty years old, and I've only just found out who my parents are. I should have known before. Especially because, in the world I'm from, not knowing information like this could get me killed.

"I'm not your biological daughter, am I?" I ask, and she turns white. Her hand shakes as she puts the cup on the small, white wooden table next to her.

"How did you find out?" she asks, a quiver in her voice that I hate hearing.

"Doesn't matter, but I need to know where I came from, it's important now," I tell her.

She looks down at her hands. "I told you once that I knew your father from university, you remember?" she asks, and I nod remembering the conversation at the castle when I had called her.

"When he moved onto my street a few years later, he had a two-year-old daughter. You," she says quietly, but I hear every word.

"I helped him with you at the start because he couldn't find decent childcare. After that, I fell in love with him all over again and you as well. He never felt that way for me. Your father was in love with your mother, he talked of her all the time. Her name was Isa," she says.

"He never told me where she went, and he wouldn't tell me anything other than stories of how they met, how you were born. Your father's name was Joey Bloom, and your mother was Isa Bloom."

"How was I born?" I ask her bluntly.

"Joey said it was in the middle of winter in Scotland. The coldest winter in years, and they were trapped in their house. That's why they named you Winter," she says, and I nod, unable to respond.

"Everything was quiet for two years, and then the car accident happened. I was looking after you, and Joey had left you in my care if anything happened to him," she says, looking down at the ground.

"So you adopted me?" I ask.

"Yes. I'm sorry I didn't tell you, but I just didn't know how. It was easier not to tell you the truth," she admits with a slight sob.

"Didn't you think I had a right to know?" I ask, getting angry.

"Yes," she whispers and runs out of the room in tears. I hear her bedroom door slam shut.

"At least I know," I say to Atti. Neither of us says anything for a while. I angrily wipe away my tears.

"Go after her and tell her you love her, Winter. That woman brought up a child who wasn't hers, for a man who never loved her back. It would be a mistake for us to leave now," he says, and I nod, knowing he's right.

I go up the stairs, passing my old room as I go. I glance at the pink walls and the shelf full of trophies I won at singing competitions over the years. The awards in self-defence sit next to them. I push the door open and smile at the pictures of Alex and me all over the mirror. I was so happy growing up here; she was never a bad mum to me. I can't imagine the position she must have been put in. I close the door and go to my mum's room and knock.

"Mum." She doesn't answer, but I go in when I hear her moving. She has pulled a few boxes out of the cupboard and picks a smaller, black box out of it. Her room is simple with a small double bed, with blue sheets and matching blue curtains. The room smells like her, and it comforts me, despite the reasons we are here.

"Joey was a good man, but he would tell me all these stories of witches, werewolves, angels, and vampires. He even believed goddesses and demons existed," she says and sits on the end of her bed. I don't say a word as I sit next to her.

"I thought he was mad, but he was so sure they existed. In his will, he wrote me this letter," she hands me a blue envelope. I pull out a letter; it's old and slightly yellowed. The ends are creased like it's been read a few times. I start reading, realising that this is my dad's handwriting:

Dearest Daniella,

When we met in university, I knew you would be a great friend to me. Winter is so very young as I come back into your life, and I know if you're reading this that our past has caught up to us.

Winter is half human; her mother was half demon and half goddess. Isa could do amazing things: control animals and make people do what she wanted with only words. She saw little of the future but enough to keep herself safe over the years. Isa could also call people into her dreams; she used to bring me into hers all the time just to see me. Even as I write this, and she is miles away from me, she visited me last night. I know she wants to visit Winter, but she won't; she misses her too much, and she is still so young.

Isa told me her mother was a goddess, and she created animals. She could see the future of her line, and the humans worshipped her. She said a true goddess can live for thousands of years, and Isa was five hundred years old when we met. I know you won't believe me, but trust me on this. Winter needs to be trained, taught some self-defence for her future, and when the time is right, please show her this letter.

My sweet little Winter, the little girl who I just tucked

into bed after reading The Princess and the Pea *to for the millionth time, I love you.*

I love you so much, Winter Isa Bloom.

The moment I saw your beautiful face in your mother's arms, I knew I would do anything for you.

Your mother loved you dearly, but I was scared of her power. I'm sure you will be as powerful as she was, and she would have done anything to be with you. You look so much like her.

Isa spent her whole life on the run from her father, and never really got close to anyone because of him. We were blessed with you five years after we met, and your mother was so happy. Your middle name is her name. Her name is also like her mother's, Elissa. She thought it was nice to keep the name. She never knew her mother, as she died three years after she was born. Her protector was also killed many years later, but she escaped.

Isa said she loved me from the first time we met, when I knocked her over in a park. It's also the last place I saw your mother, when I had to run with you and give you a chance for a normal human life.

Isa once told me a prophecy about you, a very old one that her mother said. She said every supernatural heard the prophecy when she spoke it, and now everyone is fearful of it.

They shouldn't be.

You will raise them all up and keep them safe.

I love you, my sweet little girl.
Goodbye,
Dad.

I wipe my tears away as I put the letter down, and my mum hands me a black box. It's smooth and deep; it's also a little heavy.

"I could never open it, it had a note on it saying only you could," she says. I pull the lid up and it lets me, easily.

Inside is a crown, a massive white gem is held in the middle, and the rest is a soft, silver colour. There are four little gems inside the twirls holding the main gem up. There are red, green, white and black. The crown is powerful, I can feel it, and it wants me to hold it. It's like it's connected to me.

The crown glows blue as I touch it, the power spreading over me, and I quickly move my hand away and snap the box shut.

"A crown," my mum whispers, watching me as I look over at her. I look at my hand; hell, my whole body is glowing blue. I guess the cat's out of the bag, or more the glowing Smurf, in my case.

"Why did you change my middle name as well

as my last?" I ask because I never had a middle name.

"It was part of your father's demands, so I could have custody of you. I think it was another way of keeping you safe," she says sadly.

"Thank you," I say and put the box down. I move closer to my mum and hug her, she doesn't move to respond for a while, but then she slips her arms around me.

"What for?" she eventually mumbles.

"Being my mum, not leaving me when most people would have. You're always going to be my mum; blood does not matter to me," I tell her. It's true, it doesn't.

"Oh, Winter," she sobs. I hold her close for what seems like a long time. When we break apart, I notice Atti by the door. Atti looks at the box on the bed and back at me, a slight crease appearing in his forehead. I wonder if he can feel the power of that crown, too.

"The things your father talked about are true, aren't they?" she asks, looking at Atti and then back at me. I simply nod.

"It's hard to believe that all those things exist," she says quietly, and Atti chuckles as he walks into the room. He stops at the pot of flowers near mum's bed. Atti's hand glows a little green as he touches the flowers and they start growing fast. He stops when the plant, which had one flower, now has dozens.

"What are you?" my mom asks. She isn't scared, no, her face is just wondrous.

"A witch," he says and does a little bow.

"Okay," my mum says and grips my hand tightly. We don't say anything as she stares at me; she read the letter and knows what I am, too.

"Can you both stay for some lunch?" my mum asks after an uncomfortable silence.

"Yes," Atti answers, and I nod.

"Keep the box and letter. They were always yours, Winter," she says, and I pick them both up. The worn letter being the last thing I had from my father, and the crown from my mother.

"What's in the box?" Atti asks as we walk out, and he goes to put his hand on the box, but I pull it away.

"An heirloom I won't be using for a while," I respond and look down at the black box. It feels like my future is inside it and already made up before I have chosen anything.

It's a crown for a queen, and a queen is what I am.

CHAPTER 5

WYATT

"Wyatt, there has been news," Jaxson says, stomping into the room where I was sitting with Winter quietly. Winter looks up with a smile at Jaxson. The quiet is ruined because Jaxson doesn't know the meaning of it; he never sits fucking still for more than a second. It used to drive me mad as a kid, it still pisses me off now.

"Yes?" I ask him.

"Two of my wolves who watch the old castle say there are vampires in it. They have just returned to the pack to tell me."

"Where's Atti?" I ask, standing up. Winter holds my hand and smiles up at me. She is just as happy as I am that there are survivors.

"Coming," Jaxson says, and the door slams open as Atti walks in the bedroom.

"Come on, then, let's go and check it out. Here," Atti throws a sword to me and one to Jaxson. We both hold them at our sides as we walk over to Atti.

"I'm coming," Winter says with her hands on her hips as she stares us down.

"No, sweetheart, we don't know what we are walking into," I tell her, and she glares at me as her golden skin starts glowing blue, like it always does when she gets mad these days. Her beautiful eyes grow even more stunning as they glow a soft silver. Winter is stunning.

"Not happening, lass."

"Atti?" she pleads after she gives a death look to Jaxson.

"We need you here, someone to protect the pack and Freddy. Who better than their queen?" Atti says. Who knew he was the smart one? Jaxson and I glance at each other, both of us wondering how he outsmarted us with Winter.

"Okay, you're right," Winter says, and the glow slowly disappears.

"Be back soon, Love," Atti says and claps a hand on my and Jaxson's shoulders. When we arrive at the castle, Atti makes us appear just outside. Big pieces of stone lay crumbled on the old staircase up to the castle doors. What once were two massive doors is now just an empty archway, with the doors covered in dust, laying on the ground. Fond memories of escaping here as a child sweep through me, this was the only place I can remember being happy. It's clear someone has been here, the footprints on the ground an obvious sign, and the smell of blood is another. Jaxson gives me a nod as he moves behind me. He smells something. I hold my sword close as we move into the castle.

The first room is empty, other than the massive heaps of dust and destroyed walls. I hear a tiny noise up the stairs. I jump over the five missing bottom steps and onto the landing. I land silently, feeling Atti and Jaxson following me closely. They have my back; they always will.

I stop when a little boy comes out of an arch-way, his eyes widen when he sees me, and he starts crying. I move closer, and I know he is a vampire, I can sense him. His mother comes running out and picks him up. When she turns and sees us all, she falls to her knees with her child sobbing into her neck. Both of them look terrible—wearing old, torn clothes—and they are both pale enough that I know they need to feed. Children can go around two weeks without needing a little amount of blood, but adults can't do that. I turn my head when Harold, a member of my father's council, and his son Easton come out of the room. I really hope Talen, another council member, is alive, so I can fucking kill him for what he did at the castle. Injecting me with silver is a coward's move and could have killed me. I will rip his head off for that one.

"Prince, I hoped you would find us here," Harold says as he bows.

"How many of you are here, my friend?" I ask and move closer to the woman. I offer her a hand, and she stands up. I ruffle the little kid's hair, and he smiles shyly at me.

"Four hundred of us escaped, but the rest were lost," he says, and I nod. It was my job to protect them, and I didn't. I would understand if they hated me. Whoever is left is going to have my protection and help. I don't need to be their king or even their prince; I'm just going to help.

"How are you feeding?" I ask.

"The local hospital in town, which is only half an hour away," he says as the woman moves next to Easton, and he takes her hand as the kid hides behind her.

"It's not nearly enough, and the people are noticing all the blood going missing. Most of us don't believe it's safe to leave this castle and have so little knowledge of the human world that it isn't safe to go and find food," he tells me. To say they have no idea is a vast understatement; they have no fucking clue. Most haven't left the castle in their entire lives because they didn't want to. They have always had everything spoon-fed to them. Time for a huge fucking change; like calling humans food for one. They have got to stop that shit.

"How did you know of this place?" I ask, as not many do. This is the old home of the goddess, and it's well hidden in the middle of the Lake District in England. There's a huge glamor that makes it impossible to find unless you know it's there, and even then, no one ever finds it. The only reason we know of it is because Atti's mother showed it to him. He then brought us here, and we used to come every week, no matter what. Jaxson had wolves watching the place just in case anyone ever found it.

"Those that believe in the goddess can always find her home. Your mother once told me of this place–a story really, my prince. I knew it was a risk, but we didn't have anywhere else to go," he tells me.

I nod, ignoring the pain from him speaking

about my mother. I wish she were here to guide me, and maybe she could have stopped my father's death. I don't feel grief for my father, not when I know every moment of kindness he showed me growing up was a lie. The only reason he kept me alive was for the demon king, and I fell straight into his trap with Winter at my side. It was fucking stupid and won't be happening again.

"How many women and young are there?" Atti asks, and I glance at him. *"This ruin of a castle is no place for young children, look at the boy,"* Atti whispers into my mind.

I nod at Harold, who finally speaks. I'll give him credit; he hasn't backed down in front of all these princes. "There are ten children and eight women. The rest are the guards and men that I could get out. I had an escape plan made up for weeks. Your father never told us what he was up to, but I am no idiot. I will not lose my family," he says firmly.

"I offer you my pack and help," Jaxson says, making Harold's eyes widen in shock; I turn to Jaxson, ignoring the whispers I can hear down the corridor. A few still get through to my ears, and most are in shock that the princes seem like friends.

"We need to make this place liveable and sort

out a delivery of blood to come here," I tell Atti and Jaxson.

"My prince," Harold interrupts.

"Yes?" I turn to him as he comes to my side.

"You are our king. Tell us what you wish us to do," Harold says and lowers himself to one knee, his head bent. I walk over and put my hand on his shoulder.

"We work together," I say, and Harold nods. I glance back at Atti who smiles like a dickhead at me, while Jaxson smirks.

The next two days, I stay at the castle and help set my people up. Atti took me into town so I could convince the local hospital to order in a regular delivery of the blood we need. I made a generous donation to the hospital for it, and now every week someone will bring the blood to a meeting point away from the castle. Jaxson helped using his earth powers to clean the place up, with Atti using his gifts as well.

Alex and Drake have taken over the running of the castle, while I've been ordering beds, clothes, and human food to be delivered to us. I also used my power on a local building company; they're working at the castle for the next couple of weeks.

That cost me a fortune. I'm lucky we have a lot of money saved up.

"This place is looking great," Alex says, walking into the bedroom with Winter. I stop to smile at my mate. As always, she looks happy and beautiful. She must have been at training because she's wearing tight black leggings and a small black top that stretches across her chest. I have to divert my gaze away from Winter when Alex clears her throat. I'm helping two guys sort their room out, and the beds are finally done. I've done twenty of the stupid, flat, pack beds today, Ikea does not make those things easy to put together.

"Hey," Winter says, looking me over. I'm sure I look like a fucking disaster, with dust in my hair and dirt all over my clothes. I lift the spare wood over my shoulder to take outside, and both the girls sigh deeply, making me look at them.

"You totally rock the hot builder look," Alex says, and Winter playfully hits her arm.

"That's my mate you're talking about," Winter says.

Alex shrugs, "Just saying. I'm off to find Drake, and then we are going to the furniture store to pick up another delivery of stuff."

I'm thankful for all her help, I can't stand

talking to the humans in town more than I have to. One of them spent twenty minutes telling me there was a difference in two red colours of paint. I didn't see a difference.

"Bye," Winter says, and Alex whispers something to her. I don't listen in, but the red cheeks on Winter's face tell me that I should have.

"Thank you for your help," a teenage boy says as he sits putting together a bedside unit. This is a huge change for the older vampires, not many of them are happy about it. They have gotten used to living like kings for years, trapped inside a castle with no communication with the outside world. The teenagers and children are coping a little better. They love the iPhones I brought everyone, and I explained what the Internet is and how to use it.

"No trouble," I say and hand him the bag full of bed sheets. I walk out holding Winter's hand, and she looks around. Jaxson's two wolves, who have a talent for building, managed to get plumbing and electric fitted throughout the castle yesterday.

"We found something in one of the towers," I say to Winter and walk her towards the left tower. We only just got into it yesterday because it had a powerful ward surrounding it. Atti finally managed to get in after a lot of work. The vampires stop to bow at us as we walk past, Winter blushes every time.

"What's in there?" Winter asks when we get to the door of the tower. It radiates a certain power; I can feel it now that the ward is down, and I'm not surprised that Winter can too.

"Come," I say, and she nods. I love that she trusts me completely. I open the door and walk through the new ward with Winter. It only accepts Winter, me, Dabriel, and Jaxson now. Atti doesn't need to be accepted as he created the ward and can just walk in. The stairs are high, and when we finally get to the top, Winter stops to stare.

A massive blue crystal glows in the empty room; there are no lights other than the crystal as there are no windows. A change I will make because it doesn't seem right. The light should be able to be seen from afar; the tall tower as a beacon of hope to any supernatural who needs it. I can see this castle being the home we need to unite our people and live in peace with Winter. The outside of the crystal is like glass, and the inside filled with thousands of tiny blue lights that move in a swirl. Atti has never seen anything like it; he says it's what protects the castle and the grounds.

Winter doesn't say a word, but she moves

closer. I go to stop her, but I'm too late as she places both of her hands on the stone. The stone threw Atti at the wall when he touched it, and it did the same for me. Winter just starts glowing the same blue as the crystal, the little lights inside the crystal moving faster into a whirlwind. The air in the room seems lost as it's hard to breathe, yet Winter looks fine.

"Winter?" I ask her, and she turns to smile at me.

"It knows me. It sings," she says just before she collapses to the ground. I move quickly and catch her before she hits the ground. I hold her close as the crystal returns to normal, and she stops glowing. I move down the stairs, holding her in my arms.

Atti is coming up them with a frown. "I felt something strange," Atti says and stops talking when he sees Winter, "Winter, is she alright?" he runs up and places a hand on her forehead.

"Yes, I think so. The crystal let her touch it, and I think it spoke to her. She just passed out," I say, and Atti strokes her cheek.

"I'll take you both to the pack," Atti says, placing a hand on my shoulder. He moves us, and we reappear in the kitchen of the house.

Anna is standing, washing up. "I will not get

used to that," she starts, and then she sees Winter in my arms. "Is Winter okay?" she asks, and I nod.

"I'll return and keep the work going," Atti says and squeezes my shoulder before he leaves. I watch him closely. The usual dickhead I have to put up with is gone, and instead he's serious all the time. It's not like him. He hasn't been in my room once to move my shit around.

I move Winter up to the room I've been using here; it's simple with a double bed and one dresser. I lay her on the bed, smoothing her long hair out of her eyes.

She is so innocent and beautiful. Not just on the outside but in her heart as well.

My beautiful mate.

CHAPTER 6

"*Winter, Winter, Winter needs to run. Run fast, child of winter, for the storm comes,*" *the childlike voice sings in my mind, repeating the same sentence again and again until I want to scream. I blink my eyes open and see myself standing before the very crystal I just saw with Wyatt. I think I passed out. I watch as Elissa comes into the room, heavily pregnant and with a man whose face is hidden beneath a cloak. The man is huge in his build; the cloak is split down the middle, showing off his golden chest. Elissa is wearing a purple cloak and a crown on her head, but it's not the one I've seen before. This one is white.*

"Elissa, you shouldn't be up here," the man says, his voice sounding deep and strong.

"Henrick, I wanted to check the barrier. I felt the need to.

Our time is running low," Elissa says and moves to place a hand on the crystal. She stops just before she touches it and moves back.

"We still have time. The demon bastard won't get us. We have our own army now; the castle is protected and hidden," the man says, and lowers his hood. His grey eyes are the first things I see; they look so much like Atti's eyes. They even have the same build and some of the same facial features. This man is far sterner with two long scars on both sides of his cheeks. They look very old. I would guess the man is in his late forties, but, being a supernatural, he could be hundreds of years old.

"Elissa, my sweet mate, you must rest. The baby is coming soon," he says, and she turns to him. I can't see her expression, but I imagine her smiling.

"Very soon. My water went about an hour ago," she says, and his eyes widen in shock. He stomps over to her and swoops her up in his arms.

"Oh, Elissa, you do love your games," he says, and she laughs. They both disappear, and I'm just standing staring at the crystal until I close my eyes.

. . .

I shoot up, awake in the dark room I'm in, the curtains blocking out the dim light, but I can see through them. Wyatt moves next to me; his deep breaths tell me he's still sleeping. I glance at myself; I'm just wearing the tank top from yesterday and some knickers. Wyatt must have stripped me of everything else after I passed out. I'm not as sweaty as before, but I still need a shower after this latest weird dream. Henrick must have been Atti's ancestor, another man who was clearly in love with Elissa.

I slide out of bed, pulling on the jeans that I find folded on the dresser, along with my boots. I pick the boots up and slide out of the room to find a shower. I knock on Jaxson's door before I go in. The room is empty, so I quickly shower and dress in a long blue top that says, "I'm the queen" on it. Alex thought it was a funny top, but it's the only thing clean at the moment. All my clothes are at the vampire castle, so I'm not getting them back. I find some new leggings and some socks in a bag by the door. After slipping my boots on and plaiting my hair, I leave the room to find some food. I bump into Dabriel as he walks out of the kitchen. I laugh as I nearly fall over, and he picks me up. He looks normal, well as much as he can be when he is seriously hot. His white hair is down, shaping his face. It stops near his shoulders. He's wearing jeans and a tight black shirt; the black stands out against his large, white wings. They look white, but if you get closer, you can see the silver, shiny strands in the feathers. His hair has a little of the silver in it too, like highlights.

"Hey, you," he smiles at me. I gasp when he kisses me before I can say anything, his hand sliding behind my neck as he pulls me closer.

"So gross," Freddy's voice comes from behind me, and I giggle as Dabriel leans back with me still in his arms.

"You'll like girls one day," Dabriel says, and I turn in time to see Freddy roll his eyes.

"That's what bedrooms with locked doors are for," he says, and I feel like I'm about to get a lecture from a nine-year-old. Should he even know about this stuff?

"Yes, locking you in your room alone sounds like a brilliant plan," Dabriel mutters. I chuckle and shake my head.

"I'm a wolf, I'll just break the door," Freddy says with a smirk. A smirk much like his father's when he is being an asshole.

"We could tie him up and gag him," Jaxson says, coming into the corridor and ruffling Freddy's hair. Jaxson has just jeans on again, foregoing a shirt, so his chest is on full display. I swear these men are trying to kill me by setting my hormones on fire.

"You wouldn't," Freddy glares at him and shoves his hand away.

"I will if you don't go and tidy that room like I asked you to last week. I want your washing down-stairs in ten minutes as well, or I'll start your training an hour early, for a week," Jaxson says, crossing his arms. If I thought dad mode was hot on Wyatt, Jaxson gives him competition.

"I don't want to," Freddy growls.

"Two weeks?" Jaxson says, growling far louder and scarier.

"Fine," Freddy says and stomps out of the room. Dabriel and I can't help the laughs that escape. Jaxson just smiles at us both.

"Let me cook for you, lass," Jaxson says.

"I have already cooked, I was just coming to find Winter when she found me," Dabriel says and turns me towards the door. I walk in and see that he has cooked pancakes and has lots of different fruits spread around the table.

"Thank you," I say as I lean up to kiss his cheek and walk over to the table.

"Where are Atti and Anna today?" I ask.

"Anna is out on a walk. The pack loves to see pregnant wolves. There aren't many. They are all saying that the goddess is blessing us again as there have been more pregnancies," Jaxson tells me. When I widen my eyes in disbelief, Jaxson continues. "There have been seven newly pregnant wolves in the last two months, far more than there have ever been," Jaxson piles a plate full of pancakes. I get two and some strawberries.

"That could be just luck," I say.

"No, lass, it's not. You're the goddess's granddaughter; people always believed the two goddess sisters brought luck to the people. She did create them after all. The pregnancies are a blessing," Jaxson says. All this talk of the goddess just reminds me of the dream last night. Elissa was pregnant with a half demon baby, that couldn't be good luck for her, considering the demon king wanted to kill her.

"It's true. Wyatt said there were four more vampire pregnancies confirmed in the months following you coming into our lives. We all believe you bring the supernatural race some form of good luck." Dabriel says.

"I don't agree, but I am not going to argue about it when there is chocolate sauce for my pancakes. Some things have to come first," I say with a grin, and Jaxson grabs the chocolate sauce before I get it. He holds it up and smirks at me.

"I'm not saying 'please', you jackass," I say with an angry glare.

"I want a kiss this time," he laughs, and I shake my head.

"I don't believe you deserve one. No one should come between a woman and her chocolate. No matter how hot they are," I tell him, standing with my hands on my hips.

"How about I take this chocolate sauce to our bedroom and find out how it tastes on your sweet body?" Jaxson asks, making me go red.

"Err," I stumble out. Dabriel and Jaxson laugh as I stare at my plate. Damn sexy men.

"Harris and Katy's mother is expecting you over there this morning. I can't go with you," Jaxson says.

I look towards Dabriel, who nods at me.

"I'm interested in these books she has," Dabriel says.

"All sorted then, lass. I have to go, and Harris is off duty today, so I have to deal with the small pack stuff. Come to me tonight," Jaxson says and holds up the chocolate sauce. He walks out with the sauce, and I laugh.

Dabriel and I clean up after we eat our breakfast. On the way to Katy and Harris's house, we have to stop to ask a few people the way, but I eventually recognise Harris's car outside a large cabin. It's two floors and has seven or so cars parked around the sides. I walk up and knock on the wooden door. Dabriel holds my hand in his.

Katy slams open the door, pulling me into a bone-crushing hug.

"I wanted to come and see you, but everything is hectic," she says, and I hug her just as tightly. Everything we went through when we saved each other's lives has given us a bond. Plus, I just like Katy, she reminds me of Alex. I have a feeling they would get on really well, like "someone would end up hurt, and I would have to break them up" kind of well.

"I missed you as well," I say.

"And you brought eye candy with you," Katy whispers, and I laugh as I pull away.

"I'm here to see your mum," I say.

"Oh, I know. She had my dad and me cleaning the entire house because the queen was coming. She even baked you chocolate chip cookies, because she heard you like chocolate," Katy says and rolls her eyes. "Come on in so I can finally eat one of the cookies," she says.

We walk into a small corridor with wooden stairs going up. The cabin is mainly wooden floors and soft-cream walls. The corridor wall is full of pictures of a young woman and several men. There are photos of Katy and Harris as children on a man's shoulders. They look so content. Katy walks us down to the end of the corridor and through a large kitchen to a dining room. The dining room has a wooden, round table in the middle, and there are eight chairs spread around it. There is a lovely bunch of flowers in the window and big French doors that are slightly open. A middle-aged woman is sitting talking to a dark-skinned man who looks near enough the same age. They both turn when I walk in and instantly stand to bow to me.

"My queen," they say together. It's still really weird to see them do that.

"It's nice to meet you, err—" I stop talking when I realise I don't know their names.

"My name is Roger, and this is my mate,

Angela," the man introduces them and holds out a hand. I shake his hand, and Angela pulls a chair out for me. I don't want to be rude, so I sit down. The minute I sit, she offers me a cookie from a plate of them. I take one, as does Dabriel, who sits next to me.

"Can I finally have one?" Katy groans from the doorway. This is a girl after my own heart, and I grin at her with a mouthful of cookie. Damn, these cookies are good. Angela gives her the plate.

"Make sure to share them with your brother," she says.

"No way in hell, mum. He has a girl over, so they are all mine. I'm going to watch some human TV," Katy says with a disgusted wrinkle of her nose and walks out, a cookie already shoved in her mouth.

"I'm sorry about Katy, she can be–" Angela starts to say.

"A little bonkers?" I finish her sentence, and she laughs with a nod.

"I like her, she reminds me of my best friend," I add, and she smiles at me. I can see the resemblance to Katy; they have the same brown hair and large eyes.

"Here you go; these are the four books that have

been passed down through my family. They are the diaries of my great-something-grandmother. She was a maid to the goddesses, and a friend of theirs. Her great grandfather was mated to the goddess," she tells me.

"I don't understand," I say. If her great grandfather was mated to the goddess, then wouldn't she be related to her, too?

"Oh. I'll start from the beginning, it should answer most of your questions," she says, and I nod.

"So, a long time ago, when the goddess was in trouble and dying from silver, a human saved her life. The man was dying as well, and he used the last of his strength to pull Demtra into his home and stitch up her wound. Demtra had the power to do almost anything, but she could not save someone from a silver wound. Silver is the only thing that could ever hurt her, and she couldn't heal others from it," Angela says.

"The man died," Dabriel adds in, and Angela nods.

"Yes, and he asked Demtra for her blessing for his children. My ancestor said that Demtra promised to give them long lives and treat them as her own children. The problem was Demtra had trouble finding them because they had moved, and she had never met them.

She eventually found two of the sons in an old hut in the middle of nowhere. The two twin sons were not as she hoped to find them; one had passed away from an illness and another was gravely injured. The one son had only just died, so she breathed life into the man, and he came back as what are known as vampires. The other son, she pushed earthly powers into, and he became a wolf as he healed," she says; this is a far better telling of the story than what Harris said.

"I know that part from Harris," I tell her, and she nods.

"I am not aware what happened to the other two sons, but–" Angela stops when Dabriel holds a hand up.

"Please allow me to tell that story. I know that part."

"May I write this down later on? I would love to add it to the books for our future generations," Angela asks, her eyes lighting up when Dabriel nods.

"The other two sons had travelled over the seas for work. When the goddess turned up with their other brothers, neither wished for her help. My ancestor was happily married and had a child. Demtra stayed near when the other sons returned home. Later, a fire raged through my ancestor's house. The man screamed for her help when his child and wife were stuck on the highest level, and no one could get close. Demtra gave him wings and the power to heal his wife and child."

"Amazing, and the witch ancestor?" Angela asks gently.

"Time went on, and the final, youngest son found his own wife. She was said to be very beautiful, and many men in the small village were in love with her. There was one man who would watch her every move and was mad about her. The man snuck into their house and took the wife when the youngest son was at work," Dabriel says and glances at me.

"The youngest son went to ask for Demtra's help when he couldn't find her or the man. She gave him the power to move anywhere he wished, including to be able to go to someone close to him and control over all the elements to serve punishment to the man who took his wife. When he found his wife, she was already long gone, and the youngest son ripped the island away from the rest of the earth with his power in anger. Demtra blessed the earth where the wife's body was buried, and the first jewel tree grew there. The youngest son killed the man who took his wife, but he was lost in sadness. The goddess gave him a final gift, the power to make a barrier around the island and keep it for himself. I don't know anymore," Dabriel says and reaches over to hold my hand.

"How terrible, but it makes a lot of sense," Angela says.

"How so?" I ask.

"Well, it is said that Demtra didn't always have a sister. Not at the start and not when she met the sons. The goddess's sister was born many years later, no one really knows where the goddess's parents are from, or if they had any other children," she says and opens the book. She moves a few pages of the worn book and stops. "Ah here," she says and starts reading.

"Elissa is a grown woman now, no longer the young baby Demtra brought back to the castle and told us was her sister. Elissa has fallen in love with the original sons, all four of them, after her heart was broken."

"So, she mated with all the originals?" I ask.

"Yes. They all must have had several or at least one child over the hundred or so years before they met Elissa. The book tells of a gathering where

Demtra asked them all to come and see her. That's when they first met. There's another part which is interesting," Angela says and flicks through the book carefully.

"Elissa was very much in love with the king of demons. Demtra told me he thought himself a god, but he was not. Only Demtra is a true goddess, Elissa is a goddess but with a tiny amount of power. The demon king had eyes for more than just Elissa and cheated on her. Elissa found out and left. Demtra was very upset," she says.

"In my dreams, I see Elissa, my grandmother," I tell Angela and Roger. Both of them look at me in shock. "One time, she was talking to your ancestor, Dabriel. He had long white wings with black tips and hair like yours. The point is that he said the demon king could not be trusted, and he had Elissa's heart first. Elissa said she loved the demon king and all her mates the same," I say to them all.

Dabriel watches me in fascination, "You saw my ancestor and he had both black and white wings?"

"Yes," I answer.

"I heard people say that he had twins, one born dark and one born light," Dabriel tells me.

"There is one more thing that is said," Angela adds in. "Demtra gave the originals and all the descendants that stayed to fight in the castle new powers, so they had a chance of survival against an army of demons. The witches were given weather magic, the wolves given a bundle of different abilities from being able to turn invisible to talking to the earth. The angels were given a power to cause pain with a touch, and to see the past and future. The vampires were given the ability to share their life with their human mates. The vampires were also given some special powers by accident; the goddess was growing weak as she protected her sister. The goddess said it was all she could do to protect the future; she said the past was lost. I will fight to protect her, she is my goddess, and Elissa is my queen," she stops and smiles sadly at me.

"So, do you know any more?" I ask her.

"One more part, and it is a sad ending," she says and moves a few pages in the book.

"Elissa and her mates are dead, much like the rest of the castle as I write this. Demtra has a stone, which she says her blood can control and is using it to lock away the demon king. I will not survive much longer, but many have. Demtra saved many today. May the goddess never die."

"Why would he kill her and them? He loved her, or must have had feelings for her to mate with her?" I shake my head.

"Is there anything else?" Dabriel asks as I swallow the sadness I feel for Elissa and Demtra.

"No, I'm afraid not," she says and closes the book.

"I have an idea. A dark angel owes me a reading because I told him his future. If he touches you, he can show you your past," Dabriel says to me.

"Is it safe? "I ask.

"Very. I will always protect what is mine," Dabriel says and lifts my hand to press a kiss to my knuckles.

"Ah, young love," Angela says, and I smile at her with a little blush.

"Thank you for all your help; I really needed to know about this. About my family," I say.

"Oh, don't thank me; you have helped me as well. Finally, I know how all the supernaturals were created," Angela says. I smile, and she comes around the table. After she hugs Dabriel and me, she walks us out.

When the door shuts behind us, I hear, "One time. It was a one-night stand, Harris. It did not mean anything," Leigha shouts. I look at Dabriel who winks and places a finger to his lips as he pulls me closer. I hold in a scream when Dabriel spreads his large wings and flies up in the air. He lands us

G. BAILEY

silently on the other side of the roof. We can both look down to where Leigha and Harris stand very close at the back of the house, both of them looking angry.

"The fuck it didn't, Leigha," Harris says.

"I'm sure you will get over it," Leigha says and pats his cheek. Harris grabs her hand and pulls her closer; they both kiss each other in an explosive passion that makes me look away.

"No," Leigha says, and I look back to see her push him away. She stomps off into the woods.

"When you drop the cold-hearted act, come find me!" Harris shouts and storms into the house.

"He's an idiot," I groan.

"Why?" Dabriel asks me.

"He called her cold-hearted. I mean, I know she comes across like that sometimes, but I don't think she really is. She just doesn't let people close. If Harris wants her, he has to prove it. Leigha will never be with someone weak, someone who lets her walk away," I say.

Dabriel nods, "I believe I agree. To give up just means you didn't love the person as much as you thought." I lean back as his wings spread out again.

"Are we going flying?" I ask a little nervously.

"Would you like to?" he asks me.

"Maybe a little?" I ask, and he holds me closer to him. I wrap my legs around his waist as he lifts me, my mouth near his, and he speaks gently, "You only have to ask."

I scream into his neck as he flies us into the sky, and he holds me closer.

"*P*aris is controlled by the demon king," I say in disgusted horror as I watch the news. The newswoman goes on about how last night, a red ward-like wall appeared around Paris. The woman says the government is taking blame and saying it's for protection purposes. What a load of bullshit.

What I don't get is, why Paris? Why hasn't he attacked the witches or us here? From what I've heard, the new, fake queen has taken control of the city and killed all the light witches that opposed her. Now, she has complete control, and I know she was helping the vampire king to open the portal for the demons to come through. She must have gotten some power boost to be able to kill my mother and control the city. All I want to do is fucking kill her.

"What's in Paris that he needs?" Dabriel asks, but he knows none of us know the answer. I glance around the room; Winter is sitting close to Dabriel's side, his arm around her shoulder and her hand on his knee. They look mated already, they are so close to each other. Winter looks gorgeous just wearing a long, purple dress that sticks to her body and makes me want to run my hands all over her. I have pushed Winter away, not because of anything she did, but because I don't want anyone close to me. Winter, especially, because her blue eyes see straight through me.

"I need to return to my city, we need an army to stop this. I need to sort my shit out," I say angrily. All I feel is anger recently. I should have been with my mother; I knew something was wrong the last time I saw her.

"The angels might help in the war, I'll go to them after we take back your throne, Atti," Dabriel says, and I nod. "I'm staying here with the wolves and Winter," Dabriel tells us all, and I agree silently. He needs to be close to Winter. He can heal her if the demon king attacks, or he can fly her away.

"I'm going with Atti," Winter says. I snap around my head to look at her, and she stands up.

"No, don't even try to dissuade me from this," she says to me, her hands on her hips.

"You know I like it when you get mad, Love, but they're right. I won't be welcomed back," I tell her. She needs to realise it's going to be a fight from the start. The fake witch queen is fucking crazy if she thinks I'll just let her rule. I fucking wish I could get Wyatt to use his power on the witches and make them do what we want. If only Wyatt's power actually worked on witches. They're the only race he really struggles with. He can't convince me to do anything. I know he can't convince Winter to do anything, and I'm hoping that's her goddess side, not her demon side. It would be useful if he could control the demon king. I have a feeling the fake queen will be powerful. The throne is mine, and the role of queen belongs to Winter. I'll die to make sure Winter gets to where she needs to be and is protected.

"So? I should be there. I'm not a damsel in distress. Don't even try saying because I'm a girl, I should stay home," she says, pulling out the sexist card. I can't say anything. I was brought up around women, and I know when not to talk. This would be one of those instances.

"I will come as well, as your protector, so I can defend you," Leigha says, coming into the room. She doesn't even fucking look a little sorry that she was eavesdropping, again. Leigha is dressed in a full leather outfit, has daggers all over her, and is carrying a big-ass sword on her back. She looks ready to fight at a moment's notice.

"I don't think this is a good idea," Leigha says to Winter, and she raises her eyebrows at her.

"Okay, army brat, your opinion has been registered," she nods.

"I can't wait to start your training again, this was only a temporary break," Leigha says, and Winter goes a little pale.

"I'm good," Winter coughs out, and Leigha walks out of the room with a laugh.

"Brat," Winter mumbles under her breath, making both Dabriel and I laugh.

She turns to me, a serious look in her eyes as she smiles gently. "I have to do this with you. I'm at your side, always," she says, her words meaning far more than she has to say. The tension stretches between us as I look at her gorgeous face. She walks up to me and places a hand on my chest.

"Fine, but I don't like it," I finally say.

She leans up and kisses me. "I know," she says against my lips and moves away.

I sit on one side, and she holds my hand as she rests her head on Dabriel's shoulder. Dabriel switches the TV on, and we watch a show about a big group of friends. It's funny, and I wish it could take my mind off the future to come.

It doesn't.

CHAPTER 8

"Be safe, lass, I don't want to have to kick Atti's or Dabriel's ass for letting you get hurt," Jaxson says with a slight growl. The growl sends shivers down my spine as he holds me close to his side.

"You could try, and I'll leave you on the stage at a strip club, again," Atti says.

"That wasn't fucking funny," Jaxson says loudly as Dabriel and Atti laugh.

"You nearly got eaten alive by those women on their hen night," Atti says with a chuckle.

"You're such a little fucker, Atti," Jaxson moves forward, but I stop him with a kiss. These guys argue all the time about the small things, in a way it's nice to see how close they are to each other.

"I think we should be going," I say.

"Be safe," Jaxson says with a nod and lifts my chin with his one finger. He kisses me once more before I move away. I already said goodbye to Wyatt at the castle. His people need him right now, and I can't expect him to come with me. The same can be said of Jaxson.

Atti holds his hand out for me as I walk away from Jaxson. My crossbow is in my one hand, and my arrows are in a drawstring bag, tied to my back. Leigha has two small silver swords strapped to her back and daggers strapped to her leather-covered thighs. She looks like a warrior princess, whereas I, I'm sure, don't look half as good as she does. Atti doesn't need weapons; he's a weapon himself, a very attractive one to boot. Atti has his long, black cloak wrapped around him, the hood is pulled up, and I can only see his bright grey eyes as they slightly glow from what's to come. Once Atti explained it to me, I finally understood why they use cloaks with large hoods. It's because the cloak is woven with magic and blocks other witches from speaking into your mind when you have the hood up. I glance over at Dabriel; he's wearing all white again, his wings folded tightly at his sides, and a long silver sword is attached to his waist with a belt. The sword is black at the end, with swirls carved all the way up it.

"That's an impressive sword, almost as big as Jaxson's," I say to Dabriel, and the guys start laughing.

"I don't think so, lass," Jaxson gets out with a laugh.

"It's really how you use it that matters," Atti says in between laughs.

"I really don't want to sit here and compare your dick sizes, can we go?" Leigha snaps. She is in a really bad mood recently. I know why, but I'm a little scared to try and talk to her.

Her dark eyes meet mine as I giggle a little, "I didn't mean," I trail off when Atti pulls me close to him.

"We know, Love," he says, and I blush. Atti lets me go so I can move in between him and Dabriel.

They both take my hand, and I see Atti place a hand on Leigha's shoulder before his magic moves us. The first thing I see is a large room with high gold walls and smooth silver-panelled floors. The room has massive ceiling-high windows that over-look a vibrant city with mountains in the back-ground. The mountains look like they surround the city, or very large town, with dozens of sparkling trees in the middle. The houses all have different-coloured roofs; the whole city is filled with colour. It's like nothing I have ever seen. The witches' hidden city; it's so beautiful and alive. I don't have time to look much more before a massive gush of wind knocks me off my feet, and I go flying across the room. A warm arm snakes around my waist, and I slam into a hard body. I look behind me to see Dabriel flying while holding me in the air. His sword is out at his side, and he's holding me with one arm like I weigh nothing. This could be good for my ego if it were a different situation.

A bang draws my attention back to Atti, and he's glowing with a lot of different colours. His hands are on fire up to his elbows, and around ten people are on the ground, burning and screaming as he moves a whirlwind of air around them in a circle. Most of the witches aren't fighting back anymore; they're passing out or holding their throats. Atti doesn't seem to notice as he continues to use his power.

"Atti!" I shout, and Dabriel flies us over to him. I glance over at Leigha by one of the windows, just as she hits a witch on the head with the back of her sword, and he falls into the pile of three other knocked out people near her feet.

"Atti, we didn't come here to kill your own people. They are only doing their job," I say loudly when we get near him. The heat from the fire on his arms is catching my skin, causing little burns as I try to get his attention.

"Atti, please," I beg, and he finally looks at me. Atti's eyes are grey and swirling like an oncoming storm. He looks at me like he doesn't recognise me.

"I'm safe," I say gently, his eyes don't lose the stormy swirl, but his arm stops setting people on fire.

Atti looks away and waves his arm, which shines a white colour. Cold air shoots through the room, and the flames on the burning people are extinguished. All of them look unconscious, but I don't think any of them are dead.

"You could have just knocked, Atticus," a sweet-sounding woman says, walking into the room.

The woman is stunning, with long black hair that hits the floor, and it looks shiny and perfectly straight. Perfect, strong facial features make her look like a doll I used to play with when I was a child. On top of her head is a black crown with large, black stones imbedded in twirls. It draws me in and reeks of power. She has a long black dress on that reveals way too much, and a black cloak that slides across the floor as she walks. Her heels are clicking on the stone floors with every step she takes. Two more witches walk next to her, they stop on either side of her like a practised routine. They both must be witches, but I can't see anything else about them as their hoods are large and stop halfway down their faces.

"You dare to wear my mother's crown?" Atti says, his voice booming around the room. I feel Leigha come to stand behind me, her hand presses on my shoulder once to let me know she has my back. Atti's hands are still slightly shining with a variety of different colours. The woman, who I'm guessing is the new queen, watches Atti with far too much interest. I move closer to his side and rest my hand on his arm. That doesn't impress her; every part of her skin starts glowing a little blacker, her dark eyes watching my hand on Atti's arm.

"I have a deal for you," she finally says, breaking the tension slightly. I don't think the offer is for me as she stares at Atti; he looks at me once before looking back at the fake queen.

"You can be king, and I shall be queen. We only need to mate and unite our kingdoms," she offers, and she watches Atti for his reaction, obviously not caring about me at his side.

"That is never going to happen," Atti says with a small, dark chuckle.

"The demon king is going to wage war on our city when he finds us, and we need to be united," she replies, her eyes narrowed at Atti's reaction. She looks pissed.

Atti laughs deeply. His laugh is spreading around the large room.

"No," he says simply and moves to step forward.

The queen starts shaking in anger, black smoke flittering out of her fingers. "I do not wish to fight you. The battle for the throne was won in the arena. I did nothing wrong," she says.

"Then let's go to the arena. Call all of the witches, and we will see who fairly deserves the throne," Atti replies.

"No, because I am not taking your throne from you. You can still be king," she opens her arms as she speaks.

"Not with you as my queen. You will die for what you did to my mother," Atti says darkly. There's a glimpse of fear on the queen's features before she schools her expression.

"Yet, I am queen," she says with a raised eyebrow.

"What if I offer you something else?" I say, stepping in front of Atti before he kills her. I know he is seconds away from doing just that.

"The human from the prophecy finally speaks," she says.

"My name is Winter," I say, and she nods. A little of what I believe is happiness in her face as she looks at me. Why do I have a feeling that I've just walked straight into her trap?

"Queen Taliana," she introduces herself.

"A fair fight in the arena for the throne? I will fight you for the right to be queen," I say, remembering what Atti said about his mother. Apparently witches approve of fighting in this arena. I have no idea if I can beat her, but I will train every night and day to try and win for Atti.

"No," Atti pulls me back by my arm, but I shrug him away. He clearly lets me because he could stop me if he wanted to.

"To become queen, I had five fights chosen by the old queen. I won every one, and, in the last, I killed the queen. Well, nearly did, but she fled." Taliana waves a hand like it's not important.

"You fucking bitch," Atti says moving forward, and Dabriel grabs both his arms to hold him back.

"I will fight three fights of your choice in the

arena, and, when I win, you give me my crown and get out of my city," I say strongly.

"Three fights won of my choice, and I will hand you the crown," she says. A sardonic smirk on her face suggests that she isn't going to make it easy for me.

"I will fight them," Atti says, shrugging Dabriel away.

Taliana laughs. "The offer isn't for you. Winter, the offer is yours alone. The crown will be yours to give back to Atti or mate with him and rule," she says with a smile. She clearly doesn't think I have a chance. I probably don't, but I'm not giving up. I have to try. I'm no coward, and I won't run.

"No, she would never survive a fight in the witch arena," Atti says angrily.

"Deal, only if you swear on a blood bind," I say.

Atti shouts, "*No, Winter, you will die,*" in my mind.

"We don't have a choice; you can't kill her *and* every witch in the city that believes in her. We need an army to fight the demon king, not a dead one or those who are left at war with their own king," I say to him. Watching me, he stalks over, neither of us saying a word, the swirling storm of his eyes drawing me in and making me want to be close to him. Atti has never looked this powerful or frightening to me.

"I won't let you die, but I support you," Atti whispers in my mind.

Taliana waves me over, and Atti stays close to my side, his hand in mine.

She pulls a silver dagger out of the side of her dress and cuts her hand.

"I swear on my blood to give the crown to Winter if she wins the three fights I choose in the arena. She will rule," she says, and I feel the magic like a vice around my neck. It should shock me, but the feeling is not all that different from when Atti uses his magic to move us.

"One more thing," I say.

"Yes?" she asks impatiently.

"You swear to let us live safely in the city," I tell her. She gives me a disgusted look. Like I would be mad to think she would try to attack me or send someone to. I'm not mad, I bet under those supermodel looks, she is just as conniving.

"Fine," she says and swears the words I requested over the cut.

"All done. Now leave, demon child. Atticus, you are always welcome to change your mind," Taliana says, her eyes watching Atti.

Atti glares at her but lets me pull him away. Once we get to Dabriel and Leigha, Atti flashes us away quickly.

We reappear inside an apartment I've not been to before. There are four black leather sofas spread around and a massive TV that takes up one wall, and a white rug sits in the middle of the sofas with a small glass coffee table on it.

There are two doors in the room, and one swings open, looking like it leads to a kitchen. A large, familiar black cat walks in. I recognise her as Jewels. Jewels looks at us and walks past us to the sofa where she stretches out. She puts her head on her paws watching us, I'm really expecting her to go and find some kitty popcorn or something.

The tension is high when I finally get the courage to look at Atti.

He is furious.

"Atti–" I start.

He waves me away. He moves to the glass windows and looks out, his back to me, so I can't see his expression.

"I will stay close and heal you, Winter. Atti and Leigha can teach you how to fight witches or anything else they put in the arena. It's not going to be easy, but I think you're right. This is the only way the witches will see you as a queen. The wolves have accepted you, and the vampires have as well. The angels respect warriors; they are more likely to accept you as their queen if you can do this," Dabriel says. He doesn't look happy about the idea, but he isn't going to stop me. Jaxson, Wyatt, and Atti are going to be a completely different story. I don't even want to be the one to tell Alex.

"I don't know what happened back there, everything somehow got out of control," I say quietly, but I know they all hear me.

"Your ass is not dying in that arena. I will make sure you are ready," Leigha offers. Despite her sometimes cold demeanour towards me, I know she cares in her own way. Harris is right; she does have a heart.

"Thanks, Leigha, I think I can do this," I say.

"No, Winter, you were only human a few months ago, and you're not invincible!" Atti roars and turns to glare at me, his hood falling away. He looks so angry. Not calling me 'Love' is a big sign that he is pissed. Atti rarely calls me by my name.

"I'm not human; I have never just been human. I know it won't be easy, but life is not easy. I can't walk away from this, from everything, because that's what you want me to do," I say to him. It's true, I have to fight or walk away, and I won't ever walk away from my guys. I know Atti isn't mine yet, and I had trouble planning us all together in my mind at the start, but it's changed now. I want our future, a life for us all at the end of this. We won't get that if I take the easy route and just let Atti kill half the city, starting with the queen. He would never forgive himself, and we still wouldn't have anyone's respect. You don't get respect from taking the easy route; it's the hard route in life that will earn it.

"She planned all this, killing you in the arena will be the best way to prove you aren't the one meant to be queen," Atti says, his tone dark and lost.

"No pressure then," I say quietly, and Atti disappears, his stormy, hurt eyes embedded in my mind.

"Atti is just grieving, don't take his words to heart, my little wildfire. He's worried he will lose you so soon after losing his mother. I'll explain to him that we won't lose you. I would never let that happen, and I believe the goddess will protect you. You are meant for better things than dying in an arena. Let me show you the spare room in Atti's home," Dabriel says and comes over to me. I'm still staring at the space where Atti was, and Dabriel's words snap my attention to him. He gently slides his hand down my arm and entwines our fingers.

"You can sleep with me in the one room. Leigha, there's a room for you as well," he says and looks at her.

"I'll sleep on the sofa." Leigha waves a hand at the sofas; only frowning briefly when Jewels huffs. Clearly Jewels has no plans on sharing with her.

"I think we should take turns standing guard. I don't trust that witch's word; anyone could attack us, despite it. Winter should not be alone while we are here. I'll start now," Leigha says, all business in her tone, and I know she is right. The queen may not attack us, but I don't trust her not to find a way around the blood bond.

"Jewels, will you help Leigha guard the house?" I ask Jewels who stretches out her huge paws, the leather sofa creaking as she moves. I take it as a "yes" when she jumps off the sofa and comes over to me. She presses her head against my stomach gently and follows Leigha through the door to the kitchen.

Dabriel takes my hand and leads me through the other door into a small corridor with some stairs at the end. We go up the stairs, and there are four doors, two on each side of the hallway. One is slightly open, and Dab takes me into it. It's a small double bedroom, there's a bed with a pile of folded blue sheets on the end and a small wardrobe made of wood. There's also a small window, and I go over to look out. We're in a small street with a grey road in the middle. The houses are average and detached. Each one has a brightly coloured roof that matches the flowers outside their homes. I wonder if there's a reason the houses are painted in such a way. I can see from here that the mountains do surround the city. After opening the window, I only hear children's laughter in the wind and catch a very flowery scent that reminds me of how Atti smells.

The city is lovely and so unusual.

"The secret city, humans refer to it as the Lost City of Atlantis," Dabriel says as he sits on the bed, then lies on his back. I wonder for a second if it's uncomfortable for his wings to have his body lay on them, but he doesn't look uncomfortable. In fact, he looks at home; he takes up nearly all the double bed. I wonder how I'm going to sleep later, most likely on top of him. I glance at the firm muscles I can see from where his shirt has risen up, and a blush fills my cheeks.

"This is Atlantis, like the movie?" I ask,

changing the subject, and I'm actually interested. I liked that film; the Disney one was the best.

"Yes. When the goddess was alive, the city wasn't hidden, and humans were welcomed if they managed to travel over the sea. I'm unsure why the city was hidden, but I'm guessing the times when they started burning witches didn't help. You remember what I told you about the witch ancestor?" he asks me, and I nod.

"This was the part of the land he ripped apart. The jewel trees in the middle are where she was apparently buried, and the trees appeared to remember her. They are as beautiful as she was said to be," Dabriel says. I can't see the trees from here, but I remember the ring filled with the shiny trees from the castle.

"Where is the city exactly?" I ask, as I know it's not on any globe I saw growing up.

"In the middle of the Atlantic Ocean," Dabriel smirks, like it should be obvious. I shake my head with a small smile.

"How do human scanners not find it? With all our technology and boats, someone must know about this place," I say.

"The higher-ups in government know of its existence, much like they know how angels have a massive town in America that humans aren't welcome in. They are aware of the supernatural world, and cover up many of our secrets," he tells me.

"So, apparently Google Earth isn't as good as it seems," I say. I never really saw the point of Google Earth anyway; all I ever did was Google my own house. I guess I must be a little lame.

"No, it's not," he laughs. Turning slightly to face him, I watch as he gets off the bed and comes to stand close to me.

"Can I survive this?" I ask, while he looks down at me.

"I won't let you die in that arena. I'll stop it if I think you can't do it, but I believe in you," he tells me. Dabriel always believes in me, I've noticed. He's always on my side. My protector.

"Why?" I ask quietly.

"You are far stronger than you look, Winter," he says, and he leans down to kiss me.

I pull back when he stops moving, and I frown up at him as he straightens.

His eyes are completely white, and he's shaking slightly.

"Dabriel?" I ask him, I shake his arm, but he

doesn't move. He just looks in a trance. Did my kiss break him?

"Atti, Leigha!" I shout, not knowing what to do.

Atti rushes into the room a minute later while I'm still shaking Dabriel, and he takes one look at him and sighs. "I thought something was wrong," he relaxes against the door.

"It is, look at him," I wave a hand at Dab.

"It's normal. He's having a vision," Atti says and sits on the bed, his huge form taking up all of the bed as he lies back and rests his head on his arms. I don't know how I didn't notice before, but Atti's shirt is missing, and his hair is messy like he has been running his fingers through it. I get a glance at his tight stomach, pecs, and the little blond hairline that stops at his jeans.

"Winter," Dabriel says, snapping my attention to him. His eyes are back to the normal purple I love, and he looks worried.

"The first fight is with a Dentanus," Dabriel says, and Atti sits up straight in bed.

"You have got to be fucking kidding me!" Atti roars, he smacks the bed as he stands up and paces by the door. Muttering something rude about a witch and murdering a city.

"No, I only saw Winter and a Dentanus in the

arena. I don't know how it ends," Dabriel says with a worried look in my direction as he crosses his arms. He looks two seconds away from flying my ass back to somewhere safe, and keeping me there.

"What's a Dentanus?" I ask quietly. I know I'm not going to like the answer.

"A Dentanus is a dragon that's thought to be a demon. When faced alone, it can cause its victim to be consumed with everlasting terror, a vicious cycle that renders them helpless. The last one I know being on earth was when I was a baby. It took twenty witches and my parents to kill it. They nearly didn't," Atti answers me, but he doesn't stop his pacing by the door.

"This one was young, not half the size of its adult form. Winter may have a chance," Dabriel says, yet his eyes give away his lie when he looks at me. I know he doesn't want to say it, but fucking hell, it's a dragon, and I'm well, me. I might as well walk into its mouth.

"Demons are immune to silver! That includes the dragon; the only way the last one was beaten was to remove its head," Atti says and looks at me.

"Winter loves animals. Unless she plans to charm the dragon into some tea and biscuits, we are screwed," Atti says sarcastically.

"My mother could control animals, and my grandmother created a lot of them. Maybe I might be able to at least calm it down. I used to be able to calm any animal growing up; I loved them. I was training to be a vet for a reason," I say.

"A dragon is a big step up from a cat, Winter," Dabriel says gently.

"This is not happening," Atti says, shaking his head.

"Dabriel already saw me there, so it is. We need to find out what weapons work on it and fast. If not, I'm going to work on my blue power and running away fast," I say to them both. They glance at each other.

"Demons aren't weak to silver or anything I know of. This is a major concern, considering your demon grandfather likely has a large army full of demons, and we have little ways to kill them," Dabriel says.

"Then we have a week to find out anything we can. I can ask Milo. He might know," I say.

"If you can understand anything he says, other than 'more food'," Atti says, and it makes me smile a little.

"To be fair, I understood when he told me about seeing you in the shower. I believe he described your thingy bob as a large stick," I say, causing Atti to laugh with Dabriel and me.

"I think the mini-demon has a crush on me," Atti says, and I nod with a grin.

"Oh, I know he does. You do realise he has been sleeping in your bed every night?"

"That's not at all creepy," Atti shivers.

"Milo tells me all about you when he comes to wake me up in the morning. Jaxson and Wyatt think it's funny. They both said I shouldn't tell you," I laugh when Atti groans.

"Didn't know he was your type, brother," Dabriel says, and Atti chuckles.

"Nope, he isn't. We share the same type," Atti says and winks at me.

After a moment's silence, Atti says quietly, "You could die." His words are spoken slowly as he moves to stand in front of me. Atti moves his whole body close to mine, until we're touching, and I'm forced to tilt my head up to meet his eyes.

"I will destroy the whole city if you die. I will destroy the world if I lose you, Winter," he says, each word filled with an image of my fun-loving Atti losing it. It reminds me of his ancestor; how he lost his wife and literally tore the earth apart. I could never put Atti through that pain; I care for him too much. I vaguely hear the door being shut behind Dabriel as Atti and I stare at each other. Atti's sweet scent fills my senses, and I breathe him in.

"You won't lose me. We can do this; we can take back what is ours and do what is right. We will always do what is right," I say, each word a quiet whisper, but my words are powerful enough to be considered a warning to our enemies.

Atti lowers his head and brushes his lips against mine, once and then twice until all I can focus on is his sweet lips. He always kisses me like he is savouring his favourite dessert, every kiss slow and leisured, making me desperate for him–more than I can admit. I'm sure my body is telling him everything I'm thinking as I tighten my hands that have found their way into his hair. He groans as his hands slide slowly down my back, until his large hands squeeze my bum.

He lifts me, and I wrap my legs around him, as he deepens the kiss.

"Winter, we can't, not yet," he says and breaks away from me after putting me down. It hurts to see him say no, and I don't really understand why.

"Why?" I ask quietly.

"Winter," he groans and pulls me to his chest. "I

want nothing more than to strip every little piece of clothing off you and show you how much I care about you. We can't because it wouldn't be just sex; I want to mate with you. Our first time, I'm going to mate with you, and make you mine," he says. I understand. The urge to be with him is hitting me strongly too. I never imagined being with more than one person for the rest of my life, but it seems impossible to imagine a life without all of them at my side. My life is a lot longer now too, longer than I know how to deal with.

"I want to show you something. I know we have a lot of crap to deal with, and you might hate witches after this, but let me show you our city," he says and kisses my cheek. "The city and people are not all evil. I know you haven't had the best introduction to dark witches or light, but I swear that some of the kindest people I know are witches. We survived a war much like the wolves' and vampires' war, so I want to show you what we fought for," he tells me.

"I would love that," I smile, and he grins at me.

"Come on then, Love," he holds out his hand, and I take it happily.

We find Dabriel in the kitchen with Mags, Atti's other familiar. Dabriel is currently feeding Mags, in her normal form, pieces of chocolate but stops when he sees us. She lifts her big white head to stare at Dabriel until he gives her another piece.

"Not chocolate, man, she gets pissy if I don't feed it to her," Atti groans, she doesn't even look at him. I don't blame her.

"Mags loves chocolate," Dabriel shrugs.

"More than anything else, including me. She will stomp and try to eat me if I don't give it to her when you leave."

"I think I've found my spirit animal," I say, staring at Mags with love.

"It was only a little," Dabriel chuckles and puts the bar back into the fridge. The kitchen is more modern than I thought it would be. It looks brand new with black counters and white drawers. There are all the appliances you would expect, and a large coffee maker. Atti must be a coffee man. In the one corner are two massive pet bowls, both pink and have his familiars' names on them. I have to admit, that's cute.

"We're going out, I want to show Winter the city." Atti pats Dabriel on the shoulder.

"Count me in," Dabriel says.

"I think Leigha is coming too," I tell them both.

"No, she can stay and watch the house. You'll be safe with us both," Dabriel replies.

"You're telling her then," I say, and Dabriel gives me a shrug like he doesn't see the problem. He really doesn't know the warrior princess.

"Sure," he says and walks out the front door. It takes two seconds before Leigha is shouting her rejection of his idea and threatening to kick his ass.

Atti looks at me, and we both burst into laughter.

CHAPTER 9

*A*fter what felt like forever, Dab and I finally manage to convince Leigha to stay at the house. Atti said Leigha scares him and stands a distance away, letting us handle her. I will admit she scares me a little, too, but I know Atti is just being a dick. Leigha takes protecting me really seriously and demands I at least take her dagger with me. I think she feels like she will fail in some way if she isn't there to protect me. At least with the pack, I was safe, and she didn't need to worry, here is a different matter. Atti walks with me close to his side, his arm around my waist. I glance up at him, he's wearing his black cloak, and the hood is up. Dabriel is close behind, also wearing a cloak, to hide his wings and hair. It makes him look massive, with oddly-shaped shoulders, so it's not too obvious he's an angel. We walk down the quiet street; it's strange because there are no cars. Other than the one time we went camping, I've been used to the noise of roads and cars. This place is so peaceful. Dabriel moves to my other side when the path opens up. The city is slightly cold, with a hint of a sea breeze in the air. I pull my leather coat closer around me as the wind blows a little.

"Do you like the witch city?" I ask Dabriel, as we turn around a corner.

"The island and city are called Atlantis," Atti adds in before Dabriel can answer.

"Yeah, but I just think of the film every time I think of the real name, so 'witch city' it is for me," I say to Atti who chuckles, and I look at Dabriel to answer my earlier question.

"I've never been around the city. I visited Atti's house a few times, but we didn't risk coming out," Dabriel replies.

"Ah, I forgot people don't know you grew up as close friends," I reply. I glance at the house as I go past; the front garden is filled with different flowers. Some I recognise, like the roses, but some are so different from anything I've ever seen with a range of multi-colours and strange shapes.

"No, they don't; I believe Taliana was shocked to see me at Atti's side. She will take into consideration that I'll heal you after the fights," Dabriel says, and I look away from the garden at him. We move out of the way when a few witches walk past us, their hoods up, so I can't see them.

"Less talk of the fights for now, I want to be a normal tourist for a bit," I say, and Dab laughs.

"Normal is not a word I would ever use to describe you," he says, and I whack his chest with my hand. Unfortunately for me, it just makes him laugh and hurts my hand because his chest is like a rock.

I stop in my tracks when we get to the end of the street because the sight is striking. There's a paddock of hundreds of different-coloured trees with sparkling jewels hanging from them. Each one is tall, built like an oak tree in shape, and they have little crystals hanging from them instead of acorns. There are so many, more than I can see, and a grey road, which looks like it goes around the paddock of trees. In front of the grey gates that keep the jewel trees in are dozens of stalls. It looks like a flea market, like the one my mum used to take Alex and me to sometimes. The only thing that is a lot different is that the witches walk down the streets with a mixture of different animals next to them. A woman walks past with a huge snake wrapped around her arm and neck. Another witch has a polar bear walking next to them; a small child is riding on the polar bear's back and pointing at things. All the witches have their hoods up, it looks like I'm nearly the only one that doesn't. The closest stall to us looks like it sells the crystals from the trees in different types of jewellery. The stall next to it is selling different-coloured powders.

"This is so amazing," I say in wonder, and Atti chuckles.

"Those are the trees I told you of once, and this is the market. People sell and buy everything here. I told you once our people live equally, and money isn't a thing here," he tells me.

"So, what do you trade?" I ask.

"We trade our magic using the stones or we trade for work," he tells me and pulls out a translucent purple stone; it looks blue inside with dozens of little sparkling magic things. I miss the old necklace Atti gave me, even if it was just used to hide my appearance. I liked that it was from him.

"Here, this will buy you anything you want," he tells me and places the stone into my jeans' back pocket. His hand slides out slowly, and being a typical man, he gives my bum a little squeeze.

"This place is so different, is it like this with the angels?" I ask Dabriel, who is looking around, and several people are stopping to stare at us now. Well, at me, being as I'm dressed weird–in jeans and a leather coat. At least I ditched the crossbow and arrows before we came out. The dagger is out on my hip though, so I still look strange.

"No. The angels live a little differently from humans, but we aren't as hidden from the world. They prefer to just watch humans from a near distance," Dabriel says.

"Things are changing for all of the supernaturals," I say, thinking of the vampires in the new castle.

"Your Majesty, I am sorry for the loss of your mother. She was a true queen," a man says, and he bows to Atti. I'm surprised anyone recognised him under his hood, but this man clearly does. He is the only man I can see; the rest are shaped like women.

"Thank you," Atti replies with a small nod and lowers his hood.

Several other people suddenly start to notice Atti, and they bow, removing their hoods. I hear *"true king"* whispered in my mind as people look at us.

"Why are there so many women, and only one man that I've seen?" I ask Dabriel. Atti is watching the women with a blank expression; giving me the feeling he's talking in their minds.

"Males are rare here, the very opposite to the wolves. Many women decide to dedicate their lives to magic instead. The women here are amazing fighters," Dabriel moves closer as he speaks. "Just what we need in the times ahead," he whispers close to my ear.

Atti takes my hand as Dabriel leans away. We walk away from the women; more and more stop to stare at us, but Atti puts his hood up. I guess he's done with talking. Dabriel moves behind us as we walk through the many stalls. I stop when I see a stall full of wands. Actual witch wands, Freddy would love one. I nod my head, and the guys follow me as I walk over to the stall. They stop on the path as I approach it.

"Charming lady, how may I help you?" the woman behind the counter asks as I look at the wands. I glance up at her, she looks around thirty, but looks can mean nothing when supernaturals have a longer life span. Her hair is wrapped in purple cloth which matches her purple dress that has a corset at the top and fans out underneath into a dress. Atti lied, witches do wear corsets, and now she just needs a spiky hat.

"Do they do anything special?" I ask when I snap out of my own thoughts.

"They are used for directing and holding magic, the colours of the wands are a representation of the element they help. For example, the blue wand is for water and the green for earth." She waves a hand over the green and blue wands.

"This one?" I ask as I point at a white one.

"Spirit," she says, and I nod as I pull out the stone Atti gave me and offer it to her.

"Is this stone okay payment for the spirit wand?" I ask.

"A deal, thank you very much, my lady," the woman nods and takes the stone from me. I pick the wand up, and she offers me a paper bag for it. I accept and look back at Atti and Dabriel who are watching me curiously.

"Ah, to win one prince's heart is a gift, to win two is a true prize. I'm sure the queen who wins all four shall be the truest winner of all," the woman says, and I look at her quizzically.

"Thanks," I utter as she offers me the bag.

"My future queen," she bows. I quickly make my way back to the guys, wondering about the woman's strange words.

"A wand?" Atti asks with a small smile as I reach him.

"For Freddy. He loves Harry Potter, and I thought he'd like it," I say.

"Here, give it to me a sec," Atti holds out a hand. I take the wand out of the paper bag and hand it over. He holds it in both his hands, and it glows white until I can't look at it anymore. I blink, looking up at Atti when he is finished doing whatever, and he holds out the wand to me.

"I added some magic, usually it would allow someone to see a close family spirit, but that is very rare and old magic. Freddy will just be able to shoot white, harmless sparks out of it for a while," Atti says with a grin.

"Awesome," I say and put the wand away in the bag.

"That's nice of you, but is it safe to give to a child?" Dabriel asks.

"It's harmless, D," Atti laughs.

"Can I see the trees?" I ask Atti, and he nods as he takes my hand. Dabriel takes the wand from me and slides it into one of his pockets inside the cloak.

"Wyatt and Freddy aren't getting along," Atti notes as we walk towards the gates to the trees.

"It must be difficult for them both. Freddy hates vampires; they killed his mum and his uncle. They have constantly battled with them, and now one is living in his house, talking to him all the time. Wyatt and Jaxson don't believe it's best to tell him anything yet," I say.

"Poor kid," Dabriel shakes his head.

"It's a fucked up world," Atti says, and I squeeze his hand.

"I think Freddy is lucky in some ways. He doesn't know it, but he has a father who would die for him and three uncles who would protect him at any cost. I love Freddy and would do anything for him as well," I say.

"Not many people have that many people in their lives that love them," Dabriel agrees with me.

"You're kind of his stepmother now that you're mated to Wyatt and his aunt-in-law to boot," Dabriel tells me.

"You're a MILF," Atti chuckles, and I laugh. Only Atti would call me that.

"Do I want to know what that means?" Dabriel says.

"It means mother I'd like to fu—" Atti goes to say,

Dabriel whacks him on the back of the head, "Changed my mind."

"That hurt, fucker," Atti mumbles, rubbing his head.

"You should learn to be polite around a lady, then," Dabriel says. I may not be able to see his face, but I know he's smiling.

"I'm sorry, my lady, might I kiss the back of your hand as a sweet apology?" Atti says in an over-the-top, posh accent.

"Nope," I say, and they both laugh with me.

We stop at the gates; it's white and has flowers and vines shaped into the metal work. Thoughts of Freddy and everything else float away when Dabriel pushes the gates open, and I walk behind him.

A warm feeling fills me just before I hear the singing. The song is sweet and light as the childlike voice sings of peace. The voice reminds me of the one I hear in my dreams; it could be the same person. I look around, but no one else is in here, and the singing is getting louder.

"Do you hear the singing? So lovely," I say in a daze, and they both look at me like I'm nuts.

"No, it's quiet, Winter," Dabriel eventually says.

I ignore their questioning stares and walk to the nearest tree as the singing gets louder. I place my palm on the wood, and the voice sings in my mind.

I sing the words, like I've known them my whole life:

Peace is coming, like war shall rise. Winter months will see the change.
Winter shall make the princes fall,
For Winter is the peace of all.
Shall the princess who will be queen bring us peace?
The trees welcome the ancient one's child,
We welcome you,
We welcome you,
You, my goddess, we have waited a while.

I sing all the words, my eyes closed, and when I finally open them, I see I have a crowd of people watching me. All the witches have their hoods down, and they look shocked. I look back at my hand on the tree. The tree is glowing blue where I'm touching it, and I feel like it's alive.

"Our queen!" one woman shouts, and I look over at her as she falls to her knees and bows. The rest of the crowd fall to their knees like a wave until only Atti, Dabriel, and I are standing.

"My queen," Dabriel says and kneels in front of me. I watch as he undoes his cloak, and it falls to the ground letting his wings stretch out. A few gasps can be heard in the crowd, but no one says anything about the prince of the angels in the witch's city.

"My queen," Atti echoes loudly as he falls to his knees next to Dabriel.

"No, you are both my equals," I say to Atti and Dabriel. They both stand and move to either side of me. The crowd whispers the word '*true queen*' around in my mind until I can't hear how many people say it.

The trees express their happiness, and it fills me with joy as I watch everyone.

This is my future, with my men at my side.

CHAPTER 10

"*Y*ou need to get this right, Winter, again!" Leigha shouts at me as she pins me on the floor for the seventh time today. She jumps off me and stands.

"I can't beat you," I wheeze and roll over to push myself up. I'm glad we came back to the pack to train because I'm sure the witches would lose any respect for me when they see army brat kicking my ass.

"You're the daughter of a half goddess. You are part demon, and you are also part vampire. You can do this," Leigha tells me. I know she's right, but I just want to throw things at her. The past week has been like hell. Leigha demands me for training in the pack at five in the morning, every morning, then she doesn't give me even a water break until ten.

"Yes, but I can't," I pant out.

"Stop whining. Do you think your enemies are going give you a chance to whine about your problems?" she says while charging towards me with her sword. I have just enough time to deflect her blow with my own sword as I pull it off the floor. My arm shakes as our swords clash, she's circling me, and landing hit after hit with her fast speed. My part vampire side is slowing her down in my mind so I can, at least, see her attacks. My forehead is lined with sweat, and my power builds up like an inferno inside me. I try to stop it, knowing Leigha wouldn't really hurt me, but my power doesn't listen. My body glows blue just before the blue wave escapes. It goes in all directions, looking like a wave of blue smoke as it hits everything in its way. Leigha goes flying, smashing through the training room door, breaking it off the frame, and disappearing from my sight. I quickly drop my sword and run into the room. Harris is pulling Leigha up, both of them staring at each other like there isn't anyone else around, not noticing the ten people in room. Luckily for Harris and Leigha, they aren't looking at them, they are all looking at me. I raise my hand to see I'm still glowing.

"Let's try something else," Leigha says coming over to me.

"You okay?" I ask, and she waves a hand at me. I see the slight cut on her forehead, and I wince. I didn't mean to do that. My power keeps attacking her and anyone nearby us. That's why we were training outside in the first place.

"Nice to see you, Winter," Harris comes over and gives me a hug. I watch in fascination when I see Freddy fighting another boy his age. Freddy has two long swords that look too big for him to hold, yet he does—and fights well with them. The other boy has long blond hair that stops around his shoulders, and he is just using one large sword to fight against Freddy's two. They circle each other, hitting hard and moving even faster. They don't take their eyes off each other as they fight.

"They are both very impressive. The other boy is called Mich, he's the only person around their age who can keep up with Freddy." Harris tells me. Mich jumps into the air and somersaults over Freddy's head; he lands perfectly and places his sword at Freddy's neck.

"That was incredible."

"Yes. They will both be strong wolves when they are older," Harris says. Freddy and Mich shake hands. When Freddy spots us watching him, he puts his swords down and runs over.

"Hey, little wolf, awesome job in the fight," I say as he gives me a hug. I hug him back and notice that Mich has followed him over to us. The boy has really strange eyes, so I tilt my head to the side to look at him. His eyes look like someone has swirled blue and grey paint together, and it hasn't mixed. It's really nice.

"Hello, Mich, your fighting was really good," I say over Freddy's shoulder. Freddy lets me go and grins at me.

"Mich doesn't speak. He's deaf, but he understands you," Freddy says and taps his head.

"How?" I ask, but Mich answers.

"I can speak inside minds, like witches do. Thank you for your words," he says, his voice deeper than I expect from a boy his age.

"Oh, well that's a cool power," I say, and Mich nods.

"Let's go for a run," Freddy nudges Mich's shoulder, and they both run towards the doorway, where there used to be a door. I watch them both chuck their tops off and shift, ripping their trousers.

Mich is a grey wolf, the one I saw before when Jaxson was crowned. Both the tops of his ears are missing. Freddy's wolf is much bigger than the last time I saw him, at least half the size of me now. They both quickly run off out of sight.

"Everyone, your queen needs your help," Leigha says loudly next to us as Harris moves to her side. I see his hand gently brush hers. It's so sweet, and I have the urge to help them be together. I know it's not accepted, but isn't Freddy proof enough that two races can be together?

The wolves all stop what they are doing to come over and bow to me.

"Please stand in a line by that wall," Leigha says, and I glance at her with a "what the fuck" expression. Harris joins the others until they are all lined up, around a metre apart.

Leigha walks off and grabs a belt that has a line of throwing stars on it. She hands it to me, and I slip it over my head. I know where this is going, and she is bloody mad.

"I want you to throw one star at each person, just above their heads," she says, confirming my thoughts.

"Are you crazy?" I whisper harshly, and she just looks at me with a blank, unimpressed face.

"No. Just do it, Winter," she says and steps away. The distance I'm standing is at least ten metres away and every one of the wolves looks nervous. I try to give the first guy a reassuring smile. If anything, he looks more nervous afterwards. I pull a star out of the belt; it's light and made of black metal in the middle. Each end of the five star points is silver and looks very sharp.

I pull my arm back and try to calm myself. I close my eyes and open them just as I throw the star. The star hits perfectly, just above the man's head with a little of his hair caught around it. Harris starts clapping and grins at me.

"Again," Leigha says. I move down the row of men, throwing star after star until I run out. I turn, and Leigha smiles at me as the men clap with Harris.

"That is a power of yours. Proof that you are strong and in control. If you weren't, you would have killed one of them. When we are fighting, you need to let your senses and mind take over. Stop thinking about how to beat me, and trust that you will. Like you trust your power to make those hits perfectly," Leigha says. She chucks a sword at me from off of the wall as I put back the star belt. I think about her words, I need to trust my powers.

"Come on then, princess," Leigha says with a nod, and we face each other on one of the mats. I watch her closely, knowing when she is going to attack, and I move to deflect her. I pull the calm feeling to me that I used when I threw the stars. I feel myself move–faster than I thought I could– and I finally understand what Leigha means. I can't think about every move or plan the fight. I have to feel it and trust myself. I move quickly towards Leigha as we battle, but she pushes me back step-by-step with each hit. I feel myself getting close to the wall, so I throw a hard hit to her sword. I turn and run towards the wall, Leigha quickly following me. I jump, using the wall for momentum to push off, and land behind Leigha, kind of like how I saw Mich go over Freddy's head. I pull my sword up and point it at her back, not enough to cut her, but enough so she knows I've won.

"About time," Leigha turns and bats my sword away. I lower it with a grin and wipe the sweat off my forehead.

"I won't say this again, but you were right," I tell Leigha. She simply smirks.

"Why do I never hear you tell me that?" Jaxson says behind me, and I grin, turning to see him walk through the doorway. He glances at the door on the floor and back at me.

"Guys are never right, man, best learn that quickly," Harris says walking over to us. "Can I have a word?" Harris asks Leigha.

"Outside," she says and walks away with Harris following her. I walk over as Jaxson picks up the door. It's really hot to watch him carry the door like it's a bag of potatoes to the doorway and rest it near the wall. He goes into the cupboard and brings out a large toolbox.

"I'll fix this, lass. Dabriel wants to see you in the main cabin," he says while I watch him as he slowly pulls his shirt off...like a teenager discovering her hormones for the first time. I've seen him without his shirt plenty of times, but hot damn, he gets me all flustered every time.

"Err yeah, I'll get to that," I blurt out. Jaxson merely smirks at me and slaps my ass as I pass by him. I find Dabriel in the dining room, books all over the table he's sitting at. Just the top of his white wings and white hair can be seen as he leans over a massive book. I walk around the table and rest my hand on his shoulder. He takes my hand in his and kisses the tips of my fingers as he speaks.

"I missed you this last week," he whispers.

Dabriel went back to the angels to find a way to kill demons or anything that can be used on them. The angels apparently have a large library and many records; if anything could be found, it would be there.

"Me too," I sigh. Dabriel pushes the chair back with his large legs, his wings hanging over the back and spread slightly out. He wraps an arm around my waist and pulls me onto his lap. I wrap my arms around his neck, resting my head on his shoulder. We don't say a word for a while, just enjoy being near each other.

"Did you find anything?" I eventually ask as he runs his large fingers up and down my back. The effect is soothing.

"No, well, not really," he says.

"Not really?" I ask.

He sighs. "There was one book, about a bundle of weapons that could kill demons. The writer says they were Fray-touched," Dabriel says, his voice sounding annoyed.

"Fray?" I ask, having no clue what that is.

"Fairies. The writer believed that fairies exist, and that they can place their magic in weapons. These weapons can kill demons," he answers, but his tone is laced with frustration, suggesting he doesn't believe it.

"Do fairies exist?" I ask.

"No, my little wildfire. I don't think they do," he says, and I stay in his arms for a long time. If only I knew how to speak to a fairy.

CHAPTER 11

"*Hello,*" *I shout through the trees that greeted me when I opened my eyes. This place is nothing like I've ever seen. Large purple trees stretch into the bright blue skies, and the grass is a yellow colour instead of green. This place is spectacular. I watch as a butterfly the size of a cat flies past me, the wings filled with bright colours. This is a dream, but I don't see Elissa anywhere, or anyone for that matter. There is nothing but the purple trees and yellow grass.*

"You called me?" a woman asks with a little laugh as she walks out of the trees to my left. She stops dead in her tracks when she sees me, giving me time to look at her.

She has on a long purple dress that is split in the middle showing off her stomach and the flower tattoos that cover it. The tattoos look like marks as they slightly move; they are lilies, I think, on blue vines. They also cover all of her arms and her shoulders as well. In the middle of her forehead is a weird symbol that looks like a half moon inside a circle. Her long, strawberry-blonde hair is braided and hanging over her shoulder. Bright yellow eyes meet mine; they remind me of a cat.

"You look just like your mother. I never would have guessed you inherited her ability to dream-call," the woman says, her voice is soothing and sweet.

"You knew my mother? And what is a dream-call?" I ask her. I try to move forward, but I can't, my feet are rooted to the spot.

"Yes, I knew her very well. She would call me often after we met," the woman says, speaking fondly of my mother. "Dream-calling is rare. It's the ability to call people you want into your dreams or travel into theirs. Have you not had strange dreams before?" she asks me.

"Of my dead grandmother and her sister," I reply.

"You can call your family spirits? It must be easy for you. Have you called your mother yet?" she asks me.

"I didn't know she existed until recently," I tell her, and she nods.

"Isa will come if you call," she tells me. I'm not exactly sure I want to do that. I didn't even know that I had wanted to call Elissa and see her past. I guess, in a way, now I did, but not at the start. So how did that happen?

"I don't even know how I called you," I tell her. "Wait, who are you?" I ask quickly before she can answer.

"My name is Lily, or at least my shortened name that you may use is. I am a Fray, or fairy, as you like to call us in your human words," she tells me. I fell asleep with Dabriel, thinking of fairies and how I wanted to know if they were real. I guess I got my wish.

"Fairies exist?" I ask her. I realise how silly a question it is when she giggles. Her laugh sounds perfect.

"Demons have invaded your realm, and you question if fairies exist, child?" she laughs.

"Well," I say, and she laughs more. "Why would I call you?" I ask her.

"You need my help, and you wish for a promise," she tells me.

"How can you help me?" I ask her.

"The question is, will I help you?" she says and laughs.

"Forget it," I mutter and try to pinch my arm. It only hurts, and I still don't wake up.

"Demons can be killed with fairy-touched weapons," she tells me. The stories Dabriel found must be true. I snap my eyes to her yellow ones as she smiles.

"When you realise how much you need me, only call, and we shall make a promise," she says.

"Wait," I say when I see her walk away.

"Goodbye, Winter, daughter of my friend," she says, and

the world goes black as I fall backwards onto the yellow grass.

"She's awake," Dabriel's voice flutters through my mind as I open my eyes. He is leaning over me while I lie on a bed. I sit up, feeling slightly dizzy. I'm not in a bedroom that I've seen before; it's modern with black and white dressers. The curtains are grey and open, so I can see the mountains outside. It's Atti's house, and I think this is his room. The bed is huge, with a black headboard that I move back to and lean on. Atti and Wyatt are leaning by the wall, staring at me, and both of them look angry. I feel my hair being tugged and look up. I see Milo sitting next to my head on the headboard.

He flies over to my shoulder and kisses my cheek.

"No dream-call so far," he says.

"What?" I ask croakily and sit up. Dabriel brings me a glass of water, and the room is silent as I sip it. I feel like I'm starving. The dizziness is from me needing blood, but I just fed yesterday, at least I think I did. Everything seems fuzzy.

"So, you want to explain where you've been the

last two weeks?" Wyatt snaps. I raise my eyes to his and put the drink down on the black side unit. Wyatt's hair looks like he has just woken up, his skin is pale, and he seems angry. Our bond tells me he's worried.

"In bed?" I ask nervously, and he groans.

"You've been sleeping for two weeks, Winter. The first trial is today, and I thought..." Atti says, and his words drift off. Atti runs his hands through his hair and comes to sit on the end of the bed. He rests a hand on my knee.

"*We were all scared. It's no fun being this powerless around you,*" Atti whispers in my mind.

"The Sleeping Beauty act is getting old, and I'm going to get grey hairs at this rate," Alex says as she walks in the room. She jumps on my bed and gives me a side hug.

"Sorry. It's not like I asked to sleep for so long. I feel worn out," I say honestly.

"Milo told us you where dream walking, and we figured out the rest. Milo and Dab were sure that nothing bad was happening to you," Alex says. She's dressed in tight jeans and a white cardigan over her vest top. Her long hair is up in a messy bun.

"I saw a fairy, or dream-called her. She knew my

real mother," I say. Alex winces a little; it's weird knowing that our mum kept this from us. Alex grew up at my side, and the same woman adopted us both.

"Apparently, I've been calling Elissa into my dreams for years. It's a power of mine," I say.

"Leigha picked up on it and understood it when Milo explained," Alex tells me. I forgot that Leigha could touch people and find out their powers.

"Did you know Leigha and Harris are getting jiggy with it?" Alex whispers to me, not caring that there are three large, scary men glaring at her.

"Jiggy with it?" Milo asks, and we both start laughing.

"That's not a sentence you need to know. Wait maybe you do, mini-demons must make new demons somehow," Alex says.

"Fire born," Milo huffs.

"We have a bigger fucking problem that includes my mate fighting for her life in two hours," Wyatt cuts in, and our laughter dies away.

"I woke up just in time, then," I say.

"You haven't trained, and we have no weapons that you can use on the Dentanus," Dabriel says, shaking his head.

"I best get showered and dressed," I say quietly into the tense room.

"I need a second with Winter," Atti says, and everyone nods. Dabriel kisses me gently, whispering in my ear, "I will heal anything that happens today, but I know you can do this. Remember, I'm here for you," before walking out of the room. Wyatt just gives me a look—a look that promises that we are going to talk later—and leaves.

"There's a leather outfit in the bathroom. Before you say 'no' to wearing it, you need to, it's easy to move in, and you need to look strong out there. Jeans will not do that for you. There are also daggers that Jaxson made for you. He says good luck, and he loves you," Alex says, and I nod, feeling a rush of warmth at her words. She leaves, taking Milo with her, and Atti shuts the door.

"Don't do this, not for me," Atti says, I can only see his back as he faces the door. I don't need him to turn to know how angry and stressed he is.

"Atti, I can't walk away from this," I say gently, and he turns to look at me. The grey, playful eyes I'm used to are now stormy and dangerous looking. At times, Atti can seem big and scary, yes, but dangerous, no. Now, he seems more dangerous by the day. Atti looks close to losing it, and I don't want to see the after effects of that happening. I never realised how dangerous it is to fall in love, let alone with four powerful princes. Princes that will be kings; princes that could destroy the world if they lost me.

"Not for this, for me. I love you, and I cannot lose you!" he shouts, his fists tightly clenched together. Atti's hair is curled around his face, looking wild and unkempt.

"And I love you, so I will fight for you!" I shout back, and he stomps over to me. I expected a fast and punishing kiss. Instead, his lips move over mine slowly, embracing me with every brush of his soft lips against my own.

"Mine," Atti says as he pulls away to kiss down my neck, his hand holding the back of my neck as he steers the kiss exactly where he wants it.

"Atti," I moan when his other hand slides slowly down my body, grazing my breasts. We kiss for a long time, with me sliding my hands around his chest and into his soft hair. My neck straining to meet every kiss because of how tall he is compared to me.

"Soon," Atti says suddenly and pulls back. We lie close, both of us breathless and staring at each other.

"I love you," I say quietly, and he smiles a little.

"I will always love you, Winter. I did from the moment I saw you. The moment you told me about those kitten knickers, I was a lost man," he says, making me a chuckle a little. "I won't let you lose this, no matter what." Atti says, straightening out with a stern look replacing the carefree one I just saw.

"Where has my playful Atti gone?" I ask, smoothing my hand down his cheek.

"Not gone, just suspended," he replies gently.

"Like you've been naughty in school?" I tease him.

"I bet you were a naughty girl in school," Atti chuckles, and I grin.

"Shame I didn't have you around to spank me," I reply as I wink at him, and he laughs.

"I'm sure you are going to give me plenty of reasons to spank your pretty ass in the future," he tells me.

"Perhaps I will," I giggle as Atti laughs. I walk around him, knowing he's likely looking at my ass as I go to leave the room. I open the door and laugh as Alex falls on her butt.

"Eavesdropping?" I ask, and she glares up at me.

"She was," Milo offers and flies up off the floor to land on my shoulder.

"I made you Choco Pops cereal this morning and then gave you a bath after you swam in it. Yet, you still snitch on me," Alex says.

Milo just shrugs a tiny shoulder at her as she gets up.

"You can take your pet back, he is a pest," Alex says, and I hear Milo laugh. He clearly doesn't care about her insults.

"You love Milo anyway," I say, and she looks at me with raised eyebrows as Atti walks past us all and goes downstairs.

"I'm glad you and witch boy are happy again," she says when he has gone.

"Thanks," I say with a slight blush.

"I've said it once or twice before, but you are a lucky bitch," she says with a small grin, and I laugh. She isn't wrong.

"If you take photos of all those guys topless and put them in one of those calendars, we would make a killing," Alex winks.

"It reminds me of that time we were in the university entrance, waiting for someone to show us around on our first day, and there was that hot guy," I say, and she laughs,

"Ah, I remember, I tried to take a sneaky picture," she says.

"It was so funny when the flash went off, and you shouted shit, dropped the phone, and then told him he was hot," I laugh.

"I did get his number though," Alex grins. That she did.

"That's the bathroom," Alex says and points at the door next to Atti's bedroom. She looks at me for a second, her face instantly sobering.

"I'll be okay," I say, and she nods.

"Atti told me what your mum said," Alex says quietly. I didn't want to tell her, so I'm glad Atti did. I know she already guessed, everyone did, but it was only me that needed to hear it from the horse's mouth, so to speak.

"Mum told me a lot. There's a box at Jaxson's with a letter from my father. I want you to read it, okay? Ask Jaxson, he'll give you it," I tell her, and she nods.

"Alright, but you are not mad at mum, right?" she asks.

"No," I say, and she smiles slightly.

"I don't care about the rules of this stupid fight, but I'll personally pour water all over that witch if she hurts you," Alex says and hugs me gently.

"Water?" I ask quizzically.

"You know, that's how they do it in the Wizard of Oz. It might be a trick for the wicked witch," she says, making me chuckle.

"She kind of looks like the wicked witch," I say, thinking of the witch in question.

"Shower and then get your game on. You have a dragon to beat," Alex tells me.

"Any ideas how I'm going to do that?" I ask her.

"No," Alex says softly.

"It's alright, I'll think of something," I say.

"I love you, Win," she says before she pulls me into a hug.

"I know. I love you as well; you're my sister and my best friend," I say. Alex pulls away and pats her shoulder with a look at Milo.

"You bleed, demon stop," Milo tells me.

"What? That doesn't make much sense," I reply.

"You blood work," he says.

"You know we need to work on your English or at least how to make sentences," Alex tells him and pats her shoulder again.

"You work on food for me," Milo tells Alex, and I hold a hand over my mouth to stop the laugh from escaping.

"Cheeky little demon," Alex says, and I wander

into the bathroom, listening as she tells Milo off. There's a pile of black leather clothes and a belt with two daggers on each side. The daggers are silver and sharp. There's a small note on top with a J on it. I open it, knowing it's from Jaxson.

"*Fight this and come home*," he says. Short and simple, yet it fills me with strength.

I pull my shirt and underwear off before getting in the shower.

How can I possibly think I can beat a dragon?

This isn't a video game I can ask Freddy for tips on.

After my mini freak out in the shower, I get out and dry off. I French plait my hair and twist it into a bun. I use the clips I find on the vanity and a headband, so it's held up tightly. I don't need my hair getting burnt off.

The clothes are unbelievably tight but soft and easy to move in. They, unfortunately, show off my hips, but it doesn't look too bad now after weeks of training have changed me. I feel an ache in my teeth before they slide out, reminding me I need to feed. I glance at myself in the mirror. Everything about me looks different. Even if you look past the slight blue glow and the silver eyes I have going on, I still look strange. I don't look human any more, my hair is too straight, and my face is too smooth.

The door is opened behind me, and Dabriel comes in. He shuts the door and glances at me.

"Wyatt said he felt your need to feed. Angel blood will make you the strongest you can be," he says. I'm a little shocked and nervous at his offer.

"You sure?" I ask as he sits on the toilet, his legs spread widely, and he beckons me over.

"Yes, I want this," he tells me. I hear *I want you* in my head instead of his words. Dabriel watches me closely, his wings hanging near his hips and gently fluttering.

I move over to him, hooking my legs over his as he helps me get comfy on his lap, our mouths a breath away, just before he presses his lips to mine. I let him control the kiss until the need to feed becomes overwhelming. I move my lips away and kiss down his jaw as his hands tighten on my hips.

I lick his neck before sinking my teeth into it. I don't know what heaven tastes like, I thought I'd come close to it by eating chocolate, but I was wrong. Dabriel tastes like I'd just drunk a glass of holy water right from heaven itself. He pulls me close as I feed, his hands pulling my core over the large bulge in his lap. The rocking sensation is overwhelming, and he doesn't have to do it more than a couple of times before I go over the edge. I break away to whisper his name, the pleasure taking over me.

"I can't wait to have you do that again when I'm inside of you. I've waited for what seems like forever to mate to you, Winter," he says and kisses me.

"Dab," I whisper, realising this was exactly what I needed: this release and peacefulness before the storm of the fight—one that has a high chance of me dying.

"Winter, my blood will make you stronger. Or at least your vampire side," he tells me and kisses my lips softly again.

"Thank you," I say, and he chuckles.

"Don't thank me. I belong to you, I always have," he says and kisses me before he lifts me up as he stands. I slide down his body, feeling every hard and toned part before I step away in a daze.

"Time to fight a dragon," I say, and he cocks his head to the side.

"You're scared," he says, and I nod.

He runs his hands down my arms. "Didn't I already tell you that nothing will happen to you from now on? I will always protect you, Winter," he says. There is not a slight bit of doubt in his words.

"I can't—" I start, and Dabriel puts a finger against my lips.

"You are never alone, Winter. Don't be scared," he says, his words don't expect an answer as he presses his lips to mine.

CHAPTER 12

*a*tti flashes us all over to the arena when we are ready, and by this point, I would be lying if I said I wasn't terrified. Atti holds my hand, and Milo is on my shoulder as we walk across the massive arena.

It looks like something out of Greece, with its sandy dirt floor. Hell, this place could be the copy of the arena they have there. It is made out of stone and rises high in the sky with thousands of seats. The stands are full to the rim with witches, all the light witches on one side and the dark on the other. It's easy to tell with their cloaks. There's a clear line between them of empty seats, and it's weird. The contrast of light and dark on each side is chilling.

There are very few witches without their hoods up; they are such an antisocial bunch.

There's a large metal gate on one side–big enough to let a dragon out, I suppose. Right above it are a few raised platforms, one in which the queen sits. There are two witches, one on each side–both look like they want to kill me–with their hoods down. The one to the left has short, shaved, black hair, marks all over her neck, which look like spikes, and a small green snake curled around her arm as she leans on the throne. The other woman is just as pretty as the queen. She has an innocent look about her, but as I meet her dark-grey eyes, I know she is far from it. There's just something off about her. Her long, white hair reaches the floor, and her pale-grey eyes remind me of Atti. She must be a light witch, and she also has her white cloak down. The queen isn't wearing a cloak at all. No, she has decided to wear a transparent, black-net dress, which shows off her perfect body, barely covering her private parts. She has a disinterested expression until she sees Atti. It's clear how interested she is in him from one look as she runs her eyes all over his body. I glance at my hands when I see them glowing blue because I want to throw her off a high-rise building for looking at my Atti like that. Hell, my Atti? Screw it, he *is* mine.

Atti looks over at me, and the slight widening of his eyes is all he does before looking away. Dabriel and Wyatt are on either side of me. Alex and Leigha stay behind us.

"I didn't think you would be truly foolish enough to come here. I've always thought humans were cowards," the queen says when we stop in front of her. Dabriel moves to stand next to Wyatt, letting Atti come to my side; Atti rests his hand on my shoulder.

"Said the witch wearing a crown she stole, and who is sitting on a throne that doesn't belong to her," I say loudly. The silence is echoing as she stares at me.

"Let's hope you die quickly rather than having a prolonged death," she says, but her sneer gives her away. She hopes I suffer a long death.

"That's the only death you will get," Atti says, and she narrows her eyes.

"The angel prince and the vampire prince standing side-by-side. You should have introduced yourself to me at the castle. I would have made you very welcome," she says, every word is a suggestion. Atti slides an arm around my waist when I step forward, stopping me from going closer. I have to close my eyes and beg my power to calm down.

"We are here with the true king and queen," Wyatt replies. Dabriel doesn't look her way as he steps in front of me.

"Good luck," Dabriel says, and Wyatt nods at me before he turns to walk away with Dabriel following. Alex and Leigha give me brief looks of worry before following the guys. Atti brings our entwined hands to his lips and places a long, sweet kiss on them. He moves back and bows to me.

"My true queen," he says loudly and winks at me before he turns to follow the others to where they are standing.

"Let's start," I hear Taliana say, and I look at her. Her pale complexion is slowly going red, and I smirk at her. They are mine, and I'm here to fight for them, she needs to get that.

The jealousy is clear all over her face as she leans back into her large, black throne. The metal gates screeching open makes me look down, and I take a step back when a burst of bright blue fire shoots out from the dark door. A large thud shakes the ground as the dragon shoots out of the door and lands a few metres away from me. It's huge, nearly as big as a house with blue scales covering every part of his body, except for some yellow ones that make a pattern down its back to its tail. Two large wings spread out, and his bright blue eyes lock onto mine. His face is slim, stretching down to his large mouth full of sharp teeth.

If this is his size when he's young, I don't want to see him fully grown.

"*Meal,*" is hissed into my mind by a gravelly voice, and it takes me a second to realise it's the dragon who spoke to me.

"Nope, I'm so not a happy meal for you," I say as the dragon's big wings flap once, twice, and he takes off into the sky. I look up, and I'm glad I do as he shoots a line of blue fire at me.

"Shit," I say and run out of the way. The fire manages to catch my arm, lightly burning, but not badly. I'm too worried about the shadow on the ground I can see; it means the dragon is following me. The dragon swoops low, and its massive claws wrap around my stomach, lifting me off the ground. Pressure fills my body. I embrace it, and when I can release it, I beg it to hit the dragon in my mind. I open my eyes as the blue wave hits the dragon's stomach, and he screeches in pain. His claw scratches down my arm as he lets go. I'm glad to be free but not so much when I see how high we are. I'm falling to the ground with an alarming speed, but I manage to use my vampire speed to slow everything down and roll as I land. The crowd is shouting, screaming my name and other things I don't understand.

The dragon lands with a thud in front of me, and I slip the dagger out of my belt. I know it won't work, and I don't think I can hurt him anyway; I feel sorry for him, he's just hungry. The dragon stares at me, his very intelligent eyes go to the dagger, and I throw it onto the ground in between us.

"*Princesss*," the dragon hisses in my mind. I hold my hands up not needing the dagger.

"I don't want to hurt you, but I have no choice if you hurt me again," I say. The crowds are screaming at this point, I have no idea if they can hear me. I don't even know if they want me dead or alive at this point.

"*Need food. Not hurt family of king*," he hisses in my mind. His eyes go to my arm, and I look down at it, seeing it covered in my blood. Milo's words come back to me.

Why didn't I think of it before? I'm quarter demon and of the demon king's family. I might be able to get out of this by demanding him not to hurt me. There must be at least one benefit of having messed up family members.

"Fly away," I say, and he steps closer.

"*Cannot. The witches block the top*," the dragon hisses, and I look up to see a faint, white movement over the arena. I didn't notice it before, but, of course, they have a strong barrier up. The dragon moves another step closer.

"*Winter, what are you doing? Run!*" Atti says in my mind.

"No!" I turn around and shout. I take the other dagger out of my belt and throw it at the queen. I aim it just in front of her throne, at her feet. She starts glowing black as she stands. A large falcon flies from out the skies and lands on her shoulder. The falcon is the size of a cat, with beady eyes, a large beak, and is all black in colour. I have a feeling it's using a glamor. It must be her familiar.

The arena goes quiet as I walk up to the dragon, my insides screaming to stop this and walk away. Another part of me, the dark part, loves this creature and recognises it as my own. Just like I did with Milo.

I place my shaky hand on its large nose. The scales are warmer than I expected them to be, enough that it's likely he is burning my hand. I don't move my hand away though.

"What's your name?" I ask him.

"*Demon name is long*," he hisses in my mind.

"Well, blue dragon, I'm Winter," I say.

"*Princesss*," he hisses in my mind.

"What are you doing?" is shouted across the arena by Taliana. I smile gently at the dragon, his eyes watching me, and then I turn to face her.

"Winning with peace and not death!" I shout back, my words echoing around the arena.

"That's not our way, and you cannot win unless you kill it. It's a demon," she spits out.

"Isn't the falcon sitting on your arm a demon as well?" I respond.

She doesn't answer, but her angry eyes watch me as I address the crowd.

"You expect everything to be won with death!" I shout. Silence is all I get from the witches sitting with their cloaks up.

"I am no witch. I am no human, not anymore. This is my way, and this creature does not deserve death any more than the familiars you have next to you," I say, and I see a few people remove their hoods and stand.

"The goddess wouldn't want this death. The

dragon should be free," I shout. I feel the power in my words, a power I don't recognise as it takes over me. My arms start glowing blue as I lock eyes with Taliana. She is glowing black; her hands have black smoke flowing out of them onto the floor.

"*Freedom*," I hear someone whisper in my mind, and another person says it, and another.

The witches all start dropping their cloaks as they shout the word in my mind and in everyone else's. It becomes deafening, but I stand still as I look back at the queen.

"You win this," Taliana spits out and storms off.

Atti walks over to me and pulls me into a kiss. The crowd cheers loudly, and I pull away with a little blush.

"I believe I have a dragon to return home," he tells me.

"Where is your home?" I ask, turning to meet the dragon's eyes.

"*Let me fly to where I choose*," he hisses in my mind.

"He wants you to lower the wards up there," I say, and Atti nods. I watch as he disappears, and not long after, the ward goes. The dragon lowers its head and then takes off into the sky.

"*Debt will be repaid, princess*," he hisses into my mind as he disappears from view.

CHAPTER 13

"*L*et's look at your arm, I saw it cut," Dabriel says. I pull my top off, since I have a vest top on underneath it, and show him my arm. We left the arena quickly after the dragon flew away; the witches all disappeared as well. Atti said he was proud of me, and that I did the right thing, even if I scared him. We're in the spare bedroom, I'm not sure why, but it's where Dabriel took me once we got back to Atti's house. I look down when he wipes the dry blood away, and he frowns as he turns my arm over. The skin is clean and the burn I got on the top of my arm is nearly all gone too.

"How? You're healing like an angel," Dabriel says, and he leans back.

"Don't vampires heal like this?" I ask.

"Not from a magic fire or a cut that deep. It would take at least a day. My people can make natural healing herbs and put magic into them, but even that wouldn't heal a magic burn that fast," he tells me.

"Must have been your blood," I comment, and he shakes his head.

"No, vampires have had angel blood before, and all it does is make them a little stronger," he says quietly and watches me.

"So, this is weird?" I ask, and he nods.

"What's wrong? I can feel your worry through the bond," Wyatt says, coming into the small bedroom, and Atti follows closing the door behind him.

"She healed herself," Dabriel says as he links his hands with mine, and Wyatt walks over to me. He kneels in front of me and takes my now healed arm so he can look at it.

"I've been thinking about something," Wyatt says, and he stands up.

"When Winter shared blood with Jaxson, she developed the power to aim perfectly. After a chat with Alex, it's clear she didn't always have that power," he says.

"Then when I gave her my blood, that blue power developed," Wyatt says.

"You think I'm somehow gaining more powers when I take your blood?" I ask. It makes a lot of sense. Maybe that's my power from my goddess side, as well as the animal connection, or maybe the dream-calling is.

"I'll get Leigha, she'll tell us if you have a new power," Wyatt says and walks out.

"I think the connection with animals is a goddess gift of mine, and dream-calling a demon power perhaps. I'm not sure what this one is," I say, and Atti comes to sit next to me.

"I wonder what you will get when you feed on me," Atti says and takes my hand in his.

"No idea, I don't seem to be getting the same powers as you," I comment.

"Well, Jaxson does have a deadly aim, but it certainly isn't like yours," Atti tells me.

"Yeah, and I'm pretty sure I haven't seen Wyatt glowing blue recently," I add, and Atti smirks.

"I think your demon half has some effect on that power," Dabriel says, and I turn to him.

"Why?" I ask him.

"Most demons glow a shade of blue, and I can

see their auras as well. They are blue like yours, but yours is lighter," he tells me.

"Let's have at it then," Leigha comes into the room, with Wyatt following. I hold my hand out, she takes it, and a few seconds later, she breaks away.

"New healing power, as well as the others," she says, and I nod. I knew she was going to say that.

"I guess the new power will help," I say.

"You were impressive in the arena," Atti says, and I smile slightly. I only did what felt natural.

"I can't see the next task," Dabriel says, and he looks down at me with worry.

"Faster, pony," I hear and glance towards the open doorway just in time to see Milo riding on Jewel's back. Milo even has a ribbon, and he's swinging it around in the air.

We all burst into laughter, even Leigha. That's not something you see every day.

CHAPTER 14

"Get up, and let's go out, you look bored," Atti says as he walks into his lounge. He's dressed more casually than usual, in jeans and a tight, black shirt. I wouldn't say I'm bored, I'm just seeing how many of my chocolate biscuits I can balance on Mags's head as she sleeps on my lap in her glamor. I get to seven before Atti speaks, and she moves her head. The biscuits fall to the ground as Mags looks up at me. She gets off my lap and walks out, pushing her body against Atti's leg as she goes.

"I'm not bored, exactly," I say, and Atti just smiles as he comes over and pulls me up to his chest. He wraps his arms around me and gently leans down to press a simple kiss to my lips.

We disappear as he pulls away from the kiss. When I open my eyes, I see that we are at the pack.

"Thought you might miss a broody fucker that lives here," Atti shrugs, and I laugh.

"I hope she does," Jaxson says, coming out of the front door and walking over to me. Jaxson is just wearing jeans and a grey shirt, but he somehow manages to look every bit the dangerous and sexy Wolfman I love. His hair is newly shaved at the sides; the top part is shorter, letting me see his bright green eyes. Jaxson doesn't care that I am standing next to Atti, as his hand goes into my hair and his lips meet mine. I moan as the taste of him fills my senses; I underestimated how much I missed him.

"This is strangely turning me on," Atti says, and I break away from Jaxson with a small smile.

"I really didn't need to know that, witch," Leigha says as she walks past us all. I can't help the small laugh that escapes when Atti winks at me.

"Anna's in labour, I was close to calling for you," Jaxson says, and I lean back, shocked.

"Me?" I ask nervously. Why the hell would she want me at the birth of her child?

"She wants you here," Jaxson confirms my worries.

"Okay, let's go," I say, because I can't say no when I hear a scream come from the house. Jaxson grabs my arm gently as I walk past.

"Esta is up there, she's a midwife," he says, and I nod.

"You're my mate. We don't have to argue or hate each other anymore. It's the past," I say. I can't say I like her, but she hasn't actively tried to go after Jaxson for months. He told me she is mated with another wolf she met when the packs joined. She's moved on, and the past is the past. It's not like I don't have enough enemies as it is.

"You're too nice, Love," Atti says, and I wink at him. I turn and walk into the house, leaving the guys to catch up. The two wolves at the door lower their heads when they see me, and I look back to see my guys watching me as I open the wooden doors. They look so strong standing next to one another. Atti is slightly taller than Jaxson, but Jaxson is a little wider in his shoulders and arms. I close the door behind me, and a scream directs my attention upstairs. I follow the noise until I find Anna's room. I knock before coming in, and Anna is on her side in her large bed. There's a wooden cot on one side, and a changing unit filled with things for the baby.

Esta stands at the side; her back going rigid

when she senses me. She turns to stare at me, I don't know why I feel threatened around her, but I do. I don't get it.

"Winter!" Anna shouts, and I look down to see myself going blue.

"Shit! Sorry, Anna, I can't control the glowing," I say. *I didn't even notice I was doing it.*

"Come here," she says before she screams again. I run over and pull a chair close to her bed. I hold her hand, her other is holding her stomach.

"Here, wipe her face while I see what's going on," Esta hands a cold, wet hand towel to me, and I nod as I take it. I do as Esta says, and Anna rolls onto her back with Esta's help. She checks her over.

"So close, I can see your baby's head," Esta says, and I give her a shocked look. She just looks at me like I'm an idiot.

"Push for me when you get the next contraction, Anna," she says, and Anna squeezes my hand tight as she screams. I don't dare move in the next few minutes until we hear a baby cry. I choke back tears as Esta passes a small baby wrapped in a white towel to Anna.

"A girl," Esta says, and I look in shock at the little one. Girls are so rare for wolves, and this girl is a child of an alpha to boot. She has a bit of blonde hair on her head, and she opens her eyes. They're blue, just like Fergus's. Anna bursts into tears, and I kiss her forehead.

"She looks just like her dad," I say, and Anna nods watching her baby.

"Her name is Marie, after my mother. Her middle name is Winter after you. The queen that will give her a future," Anna says, she meets my eyes, and I nod. It's the first time I realise that I'm not just fighting for a future for me; I am fighting for a future for all of the children. If that's not a reason to fight, then I don't know what is.

"Thank you," I say, and she goes back to staring at her little baby.

"Why don't you go and tell everyone?" Esta says. It's not rude because I know she has to clean up Anna.

"Okay. Is that alright?" I ask Anna, and she nods, still staring at her little one.

I walk out and down the stairs. Everyone is sitting in the lounge, and Freddy runs up to me.

"Is the baby okay? We heard a cry," Freddy says.

"Yes, you have a new cousin. A girl called Marie Winter," I say, and everyone starts clapping. Jaxson meets my eyes, and his smile is so wide, I can't help but grin back. Wyatt nods at me, his gaze watching

Freddy closely. It must be strange to talk of babies when he missed Freddy being that young.

Wyatt looks as hot as always. I notice his hair looks a mess, like he's been running his fingers through it. I kind of like it. He's a hot mess. He's dressed in jeans and a white shirt, so casual compared to what I'm used to seeing him in.

"The first girl born in two years for the packs. The first alpha girl in fifty years," Lucinda says, coming into the room, and she comes over to me. I give her a hug when Freddy moves away, and she smiles.

"I'll go and see if I can help," she says and walks up the stairs. Freddy pulls my hand and leads me to the sofa.

"Wyatt, how are the vampires?" I ask him.

"Stupid vampires," Freddy mutters under his breath, and I glare at him.

"Settling in at the castle. Others have been turning up, but it's a slow build to get the place suitable for the people. Jaxson's been helping us," he says. Jaxson nods his agreement.

"That's good. I was wondering what all your last names are, what's the baby's?" I ask Jaxson.

"Jaxson Ulrika, but we don't use last names

often. The baby's last name will be the same," he tells me.

"I know Atti's is Lynx, Wyatt?" I ask him.

"It's simple, Wyatt Reynolds. Like Jaxson said, we don't use last names often," he says.

"And Dabriel?"

"Dabriel Demetri. The royal name is as close as they can get to Demtra," Atti explains.

"Mine was Bloom. My real last name, that is," I tell them all. It's weird because it's a connection to a father I don't remember. I don't feel connected to the name, because I don't feel connected to my father, I guess.

"Winter Bloom. That's kind of strange, like your full name is a representation of the cold month and the spring month, in one. They're opposites of each other," Dabriel says.

"It sounds like a randomly generated name you would get on *The Sims*," Freddy says, and I grin at him.

"That's true. They come up with some weird names," I say.

CHAPTER 15

"So sweet," I say to little Marie as I hold her in my arms at the pack house. Marie's blonde hair is the same colour as Anna's, but everything else is from her father. Anna is sitting next to me, watching as I hold little Marie's hand. Her tiny fingers squeezing my thumb as hard as she can.

"Do you want children?" Anna randomly asks. I look up at her, thinking on her words. Anna has her dressing gown on, and she looks so tired.

"I don't know, maybe?" I say.

She nods. "I never wanted children, not in this world. It was Fergus who wanted a child."

"Anna–" I start.

She shakes her head. "I couldn't imagine my life without her now. She is the image of Fergus," she says, looking at her daughter with love. I couldn't imagine bringing up a child after losing their father; it must be so hard.

"She is," I say. I stare at the door when I hear something, something loud, and then the ground starts shaking.

"Jaxson just sent out a message using the bond. There are demons attacking," Anna says. I pass her Marie carefully as she rushes to me. The fear in her eyes is clear, and she holds Marie close.

"Go upstairs and hide," I tell her. She steps away from me when I start glowing, not in fear but shock.

"You're coming, too," she says. The earth shakes harder, making me sway a little. Anna leans on the wall to stay standing. Something is really wrong.

"No. I can't, and as queen, I'm telling you to go upstairs and hide. Please," I say, and she nods finally. I run towards the door and outside. The wolves are running in one direction, so it's easy to follow them using my increased speed.

When I break into a clearing of broken trees,

Jaxson is right in the middle, looking every bit the powerful king with his green, glowing crown on his head. He's glowing green as he holds a sword in his hand, and he swings it down onto the neck of a man. The man's head rolls off, and he disappears into a dark-blue dust. Jaxson's eyes meet mine across all the wolves fighting with the men. I see his eyebrows crease together with worry, but two more of those men jump in front of him, and he has to fight. The ground is still lightly shaking, and a hand goes around my throat. I try to pull the hand away as I manage to turn to see who is holding me. The demon man has glowing blue eyes that remind me of me when I glow blue. The man is grey, and his face is covered in blue veins, giving him a scary look. There is no emotion on his face, not happiness or fear, just blank. The hand is burning hot enough to leave a mark, and I feel for my own power as he tightens his grip and lifts me off the ground. I start glowing just before my power sends the man at my back flying in the air. He isn't the only one that goes flying, so do lots of wolves and all the demon men they were fighting as well.

Whoops.

The wolves use it to their advantage and rip the heads off of the men on the ground, turning them to dust. I fall to my knees when the ground shakes harder than before. I look up to see Jaxson, his sword in the ground at his feet, and his hand is glowing green as he holds the handle. Hell, his whole body is glowing a bright green. I can't stand up as I watch the earth split open from his sword, causing a massive crack that spreads towards the herd of demon men running towards him. They don't even notice as they fall into the hole, no screams, nothing leaves their mouths as they fall. The wolves make quick work of killing the last of the demons, and Jaxson closes the hole he created. When the shaking stops, I walk over to Jaxson. He's still staring at the place where the hole was, and he's still glowing. I put my hand over his on the sword, and he seems to snap out of wherever he had been.

"Eight," he says to me. I frown, not understanding until I hear a cry and then the pain-filled screams. I turn to see Angela holding a brown wolf to her chest, Katy is behind her and crying silently.

"We lost eight," I say, and Jaxson nods. I watch as he walks over to Angela and places his hand on her shoulder. He speaks quietly to her, and I walk over to Katy. She lets me hug her, and we stay quiet for a long time.

"I need to redo the ward, they shouldn't have

been able to break through," Atti says. I didn't even realise he was here. His eyes meet mine, but he only nods. I forgot he was coming to take me back to his house for a movie night today. I've been at the pack for a few days, and I spent a few days with Wyatt at the castle, too. The castle is improving slowly, Wyatt thinks that one quarter of the six hundred bedrooms are finally done. It's a big job, and there is only so much they can do in a short amount of time. The kitchens and bathrooms are done, which is a big improvement. Wyatt showed me the ten buildings outside of the castle. He thinks they used to be where the humans lived because they have about ten rooms in each of them and their own kitchens.

"No, we are moving," Jaxson's says suddenly, snapping me out of my thoughts.

"What, J?" Atti asks.

"The castle has the best ward. They just walked through our ward like it was nothing and started killing. They could attack us at any time here," Jaxson says.

"The castle is safer," Atti agrees. The wolves standing around us start speaking quietly.

"What do you think?" Jaxson asks me. I glance around at the wolves; most are covered in blood and blue dust. I see two men covering a black wolf with a large coat.

"It's smart for us all to be together," I say quietly. There are several wolves around us, and I blink when I see Harris push them out of the way. He comes over and drops to his knees in front of his mother and the dead wolf.

"No," he cries and places his hand on the wolf's back.

"Harris," I say gently as Jaxson stands. He moves next to Atti.

"Go and get Dabriel. We have many that need healing," Jaxson tells Atti, and he nods. He disappears a second later.

"I couldn't get here in time; they attacked near the other cabins but not as many. The weapons don't work on them; you could stab them, and they just carried on. We had to cut the heads off, and I couldn't leave them," Harris mumbles.

"No one expected you to, my boy," Roger, one of Angela's mates, says, coming out of the trees with three other men following closely. They all fall to their knees around Angela and place a hand on the wolf. All of her mates band together to mourn the one they lost.

"We move tonight after we bury our lost wolves.

We are at war!" Jaxson shouts, his voice vibrating around the trees. They seem to carry his message along with the fear that follows his words.

We are at war.

CHAPTER 16

*O*nce again, I find myself in the middle of the arena, a little scared, but more determined to make a better future for the children like Marie. Her sweet face flashes through my mind, I have to do this. I have to win. I have no idea what I'm up against, and Dabriel has tried desperately to see any part of this future. He says a blue wall is blocking his vision, and we suspect Taliana has found a way to block visions like the vampire king did before his death. Atti has tried finding out by asking around the witches he trusts, but no one is talking. Everything we *are* hearing is just rumours.

The queen smiles down at me, her black cloak wrapped around her head today as she sits alone on her throne. She's wearing a long, green dress that I can see through and a black cloak. Atti, Dabriel, and Leigha are at the sides, watching me. Wyatt is helping move all of Jaxson's pack into the castle. There's space, but it's cramped. It doesn't help when the werewolves and vampires don't get along. There have been many fights, but Wyatt and Jaxson end them quickly. Alex and Drake are working closely with Harris to keep the guard up on the castle. They run twenty-four-hour watches around the castle grounds and in the local village. We haven't sent any people to check out Paris yet. There's little point, the red wall is impossible to see through, and our magic won't work on it. The humans say technology can't get near it without exploding. So, what little photos they have are from a distance. That's good in a way, but people are angry they can't get in touch with their loved ones, and I fear that the demon king has them possessed to make an army.

I glance back at the queen when she claps her hands, and the arena goes silent. I look around, noticing that many witches have their cloaks down today, and many smile at me as I meet their eyes.

"Witches have the ultimate control over the elements. The next challenge is to see if the human can defend herself, or if she will die when the elements are used against her. Any true queen would be able to survive this," the queen's voice surrounds the arena; her sarcastic tone isn't lost on me. The crowd cheers, and the metal gates open. I look down as four witches come out. Two light witches and two dark. There seems to be one male and one female for each side. They all stop in a line a few steps away from the gate and a good distance from me. I can't see what they look like as they have large cloaks covering their bodies, the only reason I know what side they are on is because of the colour of their cloaks.

One of the dark witches, wearing a black cloak, steps forward and holds his hands high in the air.

"*Fire,*" he says into my mind, and a stream of fire leaves his hand and surrounds me in a circle. The heat warms my skin but not enough to burn. The second dark witch steps forward, she bows her head slightly at me.

"*Earth,*" she says, and the ground underneath me rises. I fall to my knees, unable to stand, as the loud sounds of the earth cracking fill my ears. The ground rises around ten feet in the air before it stops. I stand up and move as close as I can to the edge. The fire rises higher until I can't see the witches anymore, only the tops of the arena.

"*Air*," a man speaks into my mind. The fire mixes with the air and twirls up into a whirlwind tornado of fire. The tornado stretches high into the air, leaving only a small hole of sky when I look up.

"*Water*," the last witch says, and the ground shakes roughly making me fall backwards onto it. I crawl towards the edge, pulling my head over to look down just as a section all around the raised ground falls in. It's instantly filled with deep water that shoots up; I move out of the way just in time and watch as it shoots into the sky. Mixing with the fire and air tornado.

Holy shit, I'm completely trapped. I can't see the sky anymore when I look up, and it's getting harder to breathe. Or even think.

"Winter, use your power, stop this," Atti says in my head. Everything starts to blur as I call for my power. The pressure builds as fear for my life takes over, the hot water starting to scald my skin as it falls from the top of the tornado. Death by suffocation is not a good way to go. The edges of my vision are going black. The pressure of my power is building, but I can't think straight because of the fear.

"*Winter, I'm coming love, hold on!*" Atti shouts in my mind, his voice frantic but muffled to me.

My head snaps up as pressure I'm not used to

takes over, filling my body, and the blue wave shoots out of me. My feet leave the ground as a blue wave of my power hits the tornado, pushing it away. The water falls away–as does the fire and wind–as I take in a deep breath, and open my arms. My feet are slightly floating off the ground, and my blue waves are still leaving me. The last thing I see before everything goes black is the queen's shocked and fearful face.

CHAPTER 17

"*Winter, Winter, Winter,*" *sings the child-like voice. I open my eyes slowly, not seeing the child that's singing but, instead, the back of a large man standing in front of me. The song drifts away as the man walks forward towards a bed. When he moves to the side, I can see Elissa. She is sitting in the middle of the bed, covers wrapped around her. A small bassinet made out of vines is by the bed. It's the same room she died in. I glance at the man as he leans over the bassinet. He looks about forty with blond hair that's cut short. He's only wearing black trousers, and it leaves his pale chest in full view. There's a mark—a phoenix very much like Wyatt's—on the middle of his chest. I can't really see his face from this angle as he looks down, but I'm guessing this is Wyatt's ancestor, the first vampire.*

"She looks just like you, my beloved," the man says in a

gruff voice. It takes me a second to realise that the baby is Elissa's, and that the baby must be my mother.

"You say that every time you see her, Athan," Elissa says with a sigh. She looks very tired.

"And every time, it's because it's true. She is the image of you," he says in return and smiles at her. I look over just as Elissa starts glowing white. Every part of her skin glows, and Athan falls to the ground, his hand clutching his head in pain.

Elissa says nothing aloud, but I hear her make the prophecy in my mind.

The blue-sided human will choose a side.
When four princes are born, on the same day, they will rule true.
Her saviour will die when the choice is made.
If she chooses wrong, she will fall.
If she chooses right, then she will rule.
Only her mates can stop her from the destruction of all.
If the fates allow, no one need fall.
For the true kings only hold her fate, and they will be her mates.

After she speaks the final word, she closes her eyes. Athan shakes his head as he gets off the floor. He checks on the baby just as a woman in a long, red cloak comes into the room. I can't see her face or anything other than the ends of the white dress under her red cloak.

"Every person for miles just heard that, the demon king will find us," she says, her voice worried rather than angry.

"Then it's time, Demtra," Athan replies sadly and looks at Elissa.

"My poor sister," the goddess says, and she turns her head to where I stand.

"Winter, Love," Atti says, and I blink my eyes open. I'm in Atti's arms as he holds me close. Dabriel has his glowing hands on my head, and he lets go when he sees I'm awake.

We're still in the arena; it must only be moments since I blacked out. Yet it seemed like a long time in the dream-call. I didn't even mean to see that, so why did I?

So, it was Elissa making the prophecy that let the demon king know where she was and where his child was.

My mother.

Elissa must have hidden her not long after that dream, and I know she died in that room. I've seen all her mates now: Athan the vampire, Henrick the witch, Nicolas the angel, and Leo the wolf. She had mates just like me, but she had the demon king as a mate too.

I sit up slowly as Atti helps me stand on the rock we're on. I see Leigha seconds before she runs and jumps onto the rock. Warrior princess makes that look easy.

"A win," Taliana's voice drifts over to me as I stand. I turn to see her watching me as Atti grabs my arm, Dabriel holds my hand, and Leigha puts a hand on Atti's shoulder. We disappear while I smile at her, a smile proving that I can do this.

When we reappear, we are just outside the goddess's castle. I smile at a few wolves who bow when they see us, and I look around. The outside is quiet, with just the two wolves sitting outside. The castle looks so much bigger from here as I look up at it. It's made of smooth, grey stone, the parts that were destroyed are fixed, and it doesn't look like anything has ever happened to the castle. The four towers stretch into the sky, and right in the middle is the huge balcony that I spent time with Atti on. Someone has a row of flowers on the small wall that has been newly built, yet still looks like the rest of the castle.

"Let's go and find the others," Atti says. I see Harris come out of the castle and stop, not looking at us but at Leigha. I turn a little to see her staring at him as well, a mixture of emotions written across her face, but her stubbornness wins out when she turns and walks away. Harris's growl fills my ears, and I turn just in time to see him shift into a large, brown wolf. He jumps down the steps and goes chasing after Leigha.

"Never run from a wolf," Dabriel says gently.

"That's something Jaxson said once, she will be okay, right?" I ask him and Atti.

"You should be asking if Harris will be okay, Leigha is the scariest woman I've ever met," Atti says, and then chuckles to himself. "Well, other than you when I try to steal your chocolate," Atti jokes. Well, I hope he's joking. I'm not that bad.

"Very true," Dabriel nods, and I glare at him.

"You are meant to be on my side." I cross my arms.

"You nearly bit my finger off when I tried to taste that chocolate ice cream just last week," Dabriel says, crossing his arms in mimic of me.

"Ben and Jerry's?" Atti asks me, while I wince at Dabriel.

"Yes, the chocolate brownie flavour. Jaxson bought it for me," I say.

"Then, bro, you had it coming," Atti pats Dabriel on the shoulder with a laugh. I smile at them both as I feel hands slide around my waist, and I'm pulled back against a large body as cold lips kiss my neck.

"I missed you," Wyatt says into my ear.

"Me too," I say. I laugh as Wyatt picks me up, and we move quickly away from the other guys. I take a deep breath when he stops and lets me go.

"Wanted me alone?" I ask him, and he grins as he lightly kisses me.

"Yes," he says, no other explanation needed. I glance around to see we are on the balcony I was just looking up at. There's a blanket on the floor, with a selection of food and some roses in a vase. I smile up at Wyatt with a big grin.

"I want to show you something first and maybe get you some more clothes," he glances down at my leather outfit. I nod and pull my wet hair out of the bun, and undo the plait. It falls in waves as he just watches me.

"You're beautiful, Winter," he says, making my heart pound in my chest. Then he walks away to the new doors. Someone has replaced the stone ones that were destroyed with large, glass doors. I like it. We go into the newly painted white hallway; the floors are still the old stone but smoothed down. There are new lights on the walls, and the archways to Elissa's bedroom have new, wooden doors. There used to be white curtains in the past, but the light-wooden doors suit it better. They are shaped perfectly to the archway, and Wyatt pushes the door open. I walk in, and my first thought is that the room has changed so much. Where there once was a raised stone alter and stone floors, there is now an even, cream-carpeted floor. The new, arched windows are massive, letting lots of light into the room. There's a beautiful, wooden fireplace on one side and two small, white doors on each side of it. The main thing in the room is the huge bed in the middle, with a large, white headboard; it looks like it could fit at least five people. The bed sheets are white to match the white fur rug in front of the fireplace.

"We will get other things for the room, but this is all yours," he tells me, and my jaw drops.

"The four rooms next door are for each of us, they're just down the corridor, but I'm sure we'll take turns sleeping with you," he says, making my cheeks go red at the thought.

"We could live together, all of us," I say in a whisper.

"When we have peace, we will," Wyatt says to me and comes over to kiss my forehead.

"Then we will fight for peace," I say, my words feeling like a promise.

CHAPTER 18

DABRIEL

I smile at the old council member who goes on about how he is going to support me, if only I were stupid enough to not know he wants a price for the support.

"The older brother returns," the sarcastic voice of my younger brother says behind me.

"Excuse me," I say to the angel from the council whom I was speaking to. I turn to see my two younger brothers standing right behind me. Both of them are dressed in white, looking like twins when they're not. Their hair is more blonde than white, and it's cut short, not like most angels who keep their hair long. Zadkiel is the one that spoke; his light purple eyes make his narrow face seem cruel.

Or maybe it's because I know how fucking cruel he can be.

"I have never truly left," I reply, crossing my arms.

"The council feels otherwise," he smirks.

"A council you are not on nor have any control over, Zadkiel," I say. His fists tighten as the few symbols he has start glowing on his arms. I resist the urge to smirk at the weak show of power. Govad, my other brother, just watches us with distaste. Govad has white hair that stops at his shoulders; he looks more like me than my other brother. He's only a few inches shorter than me, and his eyes are darker than Zadkiel's. He hasn't spoken a word to me since I stopped him from killing another angel over a female. The fight was not needed and unfair, seeing as the other angel was not aware the female had been promised to my brother. My brother did mate with her in the end, and I offered the other man my protection. He was lucky he didn't sleep with her and make a bond; Govad would have had a real excuse to kill him then. Govad only speaks to my brother and is just as cruel. The only reason I can put up with him is because he doesn't want the throne. Zadkiel's thirst for power will be his undoing in the end, and it makes a problem for me.

"I will when I am king," he replies eventually.

"No," I say with a smirk, my skin lights up with all my symbols. A little fear shines in his eyes, but he is quick to turn around and walk out of the room. Govad follows closely behind him, and he doesn't meet my eyes. I look up at the old painting on the wall in the entrance hall to the council. It's of my father, and it's gigantic. My father has grey hair in this painting, a sign of how long he lived before he died a natural death. The narrow face and light purple eyes are just like Zadkiel's, and I look very little like him. I look like my mother, with all my father's power.

"The council will now see you, prince Dabriel," a young female angel says. She bows to me as I walk past and into the dome room the council sit in. They all watch me from their seats, each looking older than the next. The only one who is young is Lucifer, and he nods to me. He still owes me a favour for his future. I wouldn't say I like the dark angel, but I wish him to be on my side. I need a dark angel to sway the council with me.

"Why was I called?" I ask, getting to the point, so I can return to Winter. I don't wish to be away from her for long anymore. I've fallen for her, and the threats against her life are too high.

"The demons have been attacking our people, prince," Gabriel snaps out. I look over at him; he looks stressed and angry. Gabriel's hair is nearly all grey, and he sneers at me. He will never be on my side, as he supports Zadkiel.

"We can't see any attacks made by demons. We can't see them coming, and the witches' wards aren't working," Gabriel snaps out. It doesn't surprise me; I'm more surprised that more angels haven't died from the attacks. If I can't see any part of the demons' future or anything about the king, then they would not be able to see them coming. This is a shock for the angels, so used to seeing any attack before it comes to their doorsteps.

"I am aware of the issue. The vampires and werewolves are now living in a protected castle. The castle is the old home of the goddess," I tell them, and each of them stares at me with mixed looks of shock and disgust.

"Impossible!" Gabriel spits out.

"No, it is not. The castle has a large ward, much stronger than any witch can give us, and the prince of the witches has used his magic to hold it. It also has its own ancient magic," I inform them.

"What are you telling us this for?" Lucifer asks me.

"We should move our people there," I say, and they all go silent. Not one of them says a word as I meet each of their eyes.

"Our people are at war. It is now the time to come together and fight. We can win if we are all together," I tell them.

"It's only a month until we choose a king. Is this truly the conversation you wish to have with us?" Raziel asks me, and I nod at the dark angel. Raziel has always been impartial, and I hope he does side with me on taking the throne.

"Yes. I care not for a throne if all my subjects are dead or turned into demons," I tell them.

They whisper quietly amongst themselves for a long time before Gabriel speaks, "We will not work with the vampires or werewolves. The war can be won on our side," he says. I knew what they would say, but I'd hoped they would be smarter than this.

"You are all old fools who will get our people killed!" I shout out.

"Zadkiel believes that we should fight. They can be killed, but it takes a few angels to take down one. We would like it if you stayed and fought with us," Gabriel smiles at me.

"He is wrong, and our people will pay for the

mistakes of my brother's bloodthirsty nature," I spit out.

"I do not believe we should make a decision now. There is much to be discussed and a war on the way which we must defend ourselves from," Lucifer says, and his eyes meet mine for a second, knowing he is giving me time to save the angels from themselves.

"Agreed," is repeated around the council. I turn to walk out, but I hear, "Do you have any visions, prince Dabriel? Your brother does not," Lucifer says, and I stop in my tracks.

"Yes, but none are certain or of any use. I can't see anything other than blood and death in our future. I believe that we can work together to change this," I say, and I don't look at them as I walk through the doors, slamming them open. My wings spread open, and I take off out of the front doors, into the sky. I fly for a while before I see the old house I used to meet Atti at when he came to get me as a child. The house is in ruins, but it's away from humans and angels. I land just seconds before I'm knocked to the ground. I swing around and punch the person in the stomach, using my wings to fly into the sky. Zadkiel's eyes meet mine as he shoots into the air, and heads straight for me.

My younger brother was always the stupid one. My symbols kick in, and I fly down to meet him. I'm bigger than Zadkiel, so it's easy to slam him into the side of the house. Bricks fall all over the ground and around our heads as I wrap my hands around his throat. He tries to fight me off, but he has seriously underestimated me. I've always been abnormally strong.

"D, what the fuck?" Atti's voice comes from behind me, and a hand is slapped on my shoulder. I don't see anything other than Zadkiel's gasping and panicked eyes. His hands clawing my arms as I hold him down. If I kill him now, there won't be any competition for the throne. My people would have to listen to me.

"Fuck, he isn't worth this," Atti says as I look down at my brother. The guilt wouldn't be worth it, and I don't want to take the throne this way. I let go, listening to Atti's words, and stand up slowly, taking a few steps back.

"I will have the throne," Zadkiel laughs and coughs out. I laugh humourlessly, myself, as I step forward, and Atti appears in front of me, blocking my gaze from Zadkiel and his fucking laugh.

"He is an idiot, D, don't waste your time," Atti says as he places his hands on my shoulders.

"I can just about fucking see you when you're glowing like a torch man, let's go," Atti says, and it's hard not to smile.

"Fine," I say, and Atti moves us. His magic feels like being on one of those human roller coasters Atti convinced me to go to once. I didn't see the point, but Atti kissed Winter for the first time on one, and Winter loved it. Atti is good for Winter, more than he realises, because they are very alike. They both like to see the humour in life when times are getting bad. I don't know how to do that, but she still seems to like me.

"Why are we here?" I ask Atti when I see he has brought us to his house. Winter isn't here; she's at the castle seeing Alex and Leigha for the night. She expressed that she missed them and wanted some time alone.

"Boys' night," he says, and I just don't know how to reply to him.

"Pardon?" I ask, and he laughs.

"Atti means we need to chill out for one night, and Winter is safe with her friends," Jaxson comes into the lounge with two beers in his hand. He hands me one just as Wyatt comes in.

"Fucking hell, is that what you brought me here for?" Wyatt asks and takes a sip of his beer. I watch in humour as Mags follows Wyatt and jumps on the sofa next to him as he sits. Mags jumps into his lap, and he holds his hands in the air.

"You just stroke her, or do I need to explain to you about how to deal with a girl on your lap?" Jaxson says with a laugh.

"I would have said pussy," Atti jokes and laughs. Jaxson smirks at Atti and sits next to Wyatt. Mags gets up and sits on his lap as he strokes her.

"I'm not a cat person," Wyatt glares at Jaxson and moves away.

"So, we are discussing cats all night?" I ask, because I don't wish to do that. Mags is a lovely cat, but it's pointless when we have much more pressing issues.

"No. I got Avengers on DVD and beers. I'll go and get pizza from New York in a bit. You can't beat that shit," Atti says, and I laugh as I take a seat.

"Boys' night it is," I groan out.

"You guys are such fucking losers, I swear I have no idea why we are friends," Wyatt grumbles.

"Because you love my ass," Atti says with a big laugh, and Wyatt throws a book at him. "I'm just joking, fucker, chill," Atti laughs as he stops the book in the air with a wave of his hand, and a gust of air throws it across the room.

"Such a dick," Wyatt says, but he relaxes in his seat and drinks his beer.

It was a good night.

CHAPTER 19

"So, who is this guy we are waiting for?" I ask Dabriel. Atti brought us to a little café in the middle of town near the university I used to go to. The café is empty other than the waitress who brought our two teas over. I drink a little of my tea, it's nice and normal. I could be on a normal date with a hot guy, you know, if he didn't have wings. I know the waitress can't see the wings, or she would have run out screaming. I know this dark angel we're meeting is meant to be able to see my past, but I don't know who he is. Atti is picking us up here in a few hours, as it's not safe to go back to my apartment or to pack lands anymore.

"His name is Lucifer," Dabriel answers.

"Like the fallen angel out of the bible?" I ask, but it's not Dabriel who answers me.

"Yes, human, that was me."

I glance up at the man, or angel, who spoke. He is the very opposite to Dabriel. He has long black hair with dark brown skin. His eyes are a dark purple, and his wings are full of black feathers instead of the bright white of Dabriel's.

"I'm not sure I can class myself as human anymore," I tell him; he tilts his head to the side to look at me.

"Perhaps," Lucifer says and takes the seat opposite us at the small table. The bubbly waitress with blonde hair comes running over. Lucifer orders a cup of tea. It's so normal, that it's weird.

"You don't look like much," Lucifer tells me.

"Let's get on with this," Dabriel growls out. His tone is pissed off and goes with the scowl he's aiming across the table at Lucifer.

Lucifer laughs and offers me his hand over the table. I hesitate a little when I see the glowing symbol in the middle. It glows grey against his dark skin and looks like a half moon with an arrow going through the middle of it.

"I would never offer my power to anyone, let alone a human who is now a vampire. I owe my children's lives to Dabriel. That debt will be repaid, as I do not wish to have it over my head," Lucifer says.

I look at Dabriel, seeing his reassuring smile before I slide my hand into Lucifer's cold one and watch as his eyes glow black.

"*So little, how I wish I could protect you,*" *Isa, my mother, says to me. She is crying as she holds me in her arms. I'm only a toddler in this vision, with the little bit of brown hair that I have up in pigtails. I'm standing in front of her as my mother sways me from side to side. My little yellow dress matches the yellow top my mother's wearing. I don't know why I'm focused on that and not how my mother looks at me with such love that it hurts.*

I guess because it hurts to admit I miss her. I miss a mother I can't remember.

The vision changes quickly, and I'm in an empty street that looks familiar.

"We could just kill her; he won't know, and her power will keep us on earth," a crackly voice says behind me. I turn, seeing Isa on the ground. She's bleeding from her mouth, her clothes are torn, and she's watching the sky as two blue shadows stand over her. They keep flickering between real men in black clothes and the blue shadows.

"Do it," Isa whispers. The shadows hold her down, their hands over her chest, and she screams. I scream along with Isa as she dies. I recognise this dream; I had it when I was ten.

The vision flashes again.

This time, Isa is with my father, Joey. I recognise him from the dream I had before. His brown hair is like mine, and I have his nose. They're both looking at the little baby in their arms, wrapped in a knitted, pink blanket. The room is bright with a raging fire in the fireplace, and the windows to the little house are covered in snow.

"Winter, her name is Winter, and she will save them all," Isa says gently.

"I like it," Joey says and kisses her. The baby cries, and they both smile down at her—at me.

I blink when I realise we are back in the café. The waitress stands, holding the mug of tea, and stares at us. I attempt to pull my hand back, but Lucifer holds on.

"Put it down, thank you," Dabriel tells the woman. She shakes a little as she puts the tea next to Lucifer and runs off.

Lucifer finally releases my hand, and I sit back in my seat. His eyes are completely black when he finally looks up at me. They slowly turn back to purple as I watch. It's the opposite of the way Dabriel's go white when he sees the future.

"I saw other bits, but those are the only important things I will show you. The rest is small," he tells me.

"To you, perhaps; it's all I have of my birth parents. Thank you," I say, my voice a little cracked. It hurts in my chest, the feeling of those memories, of parents I never knew, but I just saw how much they loved me.

"I am sorry for your loss," Lucifer says, and he stands. "My debt is repaid, my prince," he looks towards Dabriel.

"It is," Dabriel answers. Lucifer goes to walk away, but Dabriel stops him. "I saw another child, a young one with dark wings and dark eyes. This one will need to move soon before the war takes him. You know whom I speak of, and I know the decision you will make. It's the only way," Dabriel says. I don't understand what he's saying, but apparently, Lucifer does, because he turns to face him with fully black eyes. Lucifer comes back over to the table and stands at the end. He joins his hands together, grey symbols appearing all over his skin. He has as many as Dabriel, well maybe a few less, but it's impressive. I watch as he rests his bent head on his hands.

"Latus vero regi," he says, his words deep, and I see the waitress drop a mug on the floor and run out of the shop. Yep, this freaked her out.

Dabriel gets up and places his hand on Lucifer's head. Lucifer raises his head and nods at me before he leaves. I watch him go outside the shop and just fly into the air. A few people passing by stop what they are doing, looking shocked.

"Does he not care if humans know about him?" I ask Dabriel who is pulling money out of his wallet and putting it on the table. It's a hell of a lot more than our drinks cost, but I don't say anything.

"Angels don't like humans, nor care if they see us. Not all are like that, but most are," he says. I hold his hand as we walk out of the café.

"What did he say to you? What happened back there?" I ask him.

"An old magic-filled promise. I will explain one day, my little wildfire," he says. The street is quiet, as it's Friday and in the middle of the day. I spot the bowling alley across the street, and I look back at Dabriel.

"Let's go bowling," I say suddenly.

"The human sport of throwing balls at nonmoving objects?" Dabriel asks with a slight frown.

"Yep. Scared I'm going to beat you?" I ask him, and he laughs.

"No, let's go," he answers and starts walking towards the bowling alley. Guys can't stand their ego being threatened, supernatural or not.

I catch up and slip my hand in his.

"We are safe for a short amount of time, right?" I ask him.

"You are always safe next to me, I would fly you away if there's a problem," he says like there isn't an issue.

I don't reply. I just squeeze his hand as we walk across the road to the bowling alley. The male attendant looks half asleep as Dabriel pays for our games and shoes to rent.

"What size?" the man asks with a yawn.

"Seven," I say.

Dabriel says, "Thirteen."

The man nods and looks under the counter at the rack full of shoes.

"Those are big feet, dude; I'll have to go check in the back room. Two minutes," the man shouts, and I look at Dabriel.

"What?" he asks when he sees my big smile.

"Just thinking of all the big feet jokes Alex and

Atti would come up with if they were here," I laugh.

"I don't get it," he says looking at me like I'm strange. I forget that he didn't grow up around humans.

"Oh, it's a human rumour that if you have big feet, you have a big–" I stop talking when the man walks back up with the shoes.

"Big what?" Dabriel asks as he takes the shoes.

I grab mine and shake my head. "Never mind," I laugh. I'm not answering that.

He tilts my chin up with his hand and smiles down at me.

"I know the saying, and one day you will know if the rumour is true," he says in a deeply seductive tone. I blink in shock, and he laughs as he walks over to the benches to change his shoes. Did Dabriel just trick me? I didn't know he had it in him. *It's damn sexy*, I think as I watch him bend over to put his shoes on, and I get a good view of his sexy butt in those jeans he wears when he's acting human. I like him dressed like this: he has a baseball cap on backwards, and a white shirt and boots that he just took off. I only move when he looks back at me, snapping me out of my staring contest with his ass.

I go first when we start bowling, and I knock all the pins down. I completely forgot about my perfect aim thing. There is no way I can lose this.

Dabriel is just as good as I am, and we both end with perfect scores. The place is empty other than the staff and us.

"We didn't think this through," Dabriel laughs.

"Nope, but it was fun, normal. I feel like I don't get enough of that anymore," I say, and he pulls me to his chest.

"How about I buy you lunch? I might treat you to one of those massive milkshakes I saw a photo of on the wall," he says. I can't see anything other than his chest, but I hear the smile.

"That sounds very boyfriend-like."

"Being the good boyfriend that I am, I'll find out if they have a chocolate-flavoured milkshake," he says, and I laugh.

"You are a good boyfriend, no, an awesome one," I say and lean back to look up at him. He presses his lips to mine gently before he increases the pressure. My mouth parts, and Dabriel takes over the kiss.

We do eventually get to have milkshakes and lunch, but we spend a lot of time kissing first.

CHAPTER 20

"*N*o one can get into Paris. Many people are questioning the government's excuse that it is a chemical explosion, and they have sectioned off Paris to make sure the chemicals aren't spread into the air. It all sounds made up," a middle-aged man in a suit tells the other anchor on some morning TV show. I know I shouldn't be sitting here watching this, I should be training or doing anything else, but I can't.

"This is what we are being told, but what the people are speaking of is demons and an invisible ward," he says. The humans can't see the red wall like we can, just a red blur.

"Yet there is no proof. If demons did take over Paris, wouldn't they want to take over other cities?

Demons do not exist, and what people are saying is just nonsense. There is no video evidence," the other man says. He's much older, around sixty, with a bald head and a smart suit.

"That's because everything electronic turns off when you get near. People are furious and want to hear from their families who are in the city," the man says in return.

"The government will open the city when it is safe," the older man says.

Dabriel turns Atti's TV off and kneels in front of me.

"What's going through that mind, my little wild-fire?" he asks me.

I glance at him. Dabriel is dressed in a white top that stretches across his chest. His muscular arms are on display, and the huge, white wings rest against his sides. His hair is braided at both sides and pulled back to the bottom of his head, and his purple eyes watch me closely. He is very handsome, that I've always known. Dabriel could have anyone he wanted because he looks like he fell straight out of heaven.

I'm sure that's out of a song somewhere. Or it should be. I'm glad I didn't say that out loud, that would have been a cheesy line.

"Winter?" he asks and cocks his head to the side.

"Everything is being destroyed because of me. I opened that portal and let him out. The goddess died to stop him. Yet I still let him out. I feel like I have all this pressure from that prophecy and who my parents were. My mother believed I would save people. She actually said that to me when I was a baby, and yet, I've saved no one. Paris is literally gone, and I know my dear granddad is killing the people there, or he already has, I just–" I blurt out.

Dabriel rests his finger against my lips to stop my rant. He stands and offers me a hand to get up. No words, just a hand.

I slide my hand into his, and he moves us into the kitchen where Atti is cooking Mags and Jewels chicken breasts.

"Take us to my town, to the pool, Atti," Dabriel says as he walks in. Atti takes one look at me and nods.

"Be back in a second to sort your food out, guys," he tells them both. They both are in their normal cat forms, making me think they prefer their glamors. Atti links his hand with mine and presses a kiss to my forehead as he moves us to where he was asked. I have no idea where he means.

We appear just outside a long pool inside a white building. The sun shines down on the glass skylight above the pool. The water is clear and brilliantly blue, blue enough that I know it's not normal water. The tiles look like real gold and feel cold under my bare feet.

"I'll come back in a couple of hours for Winter's training," Atti says and kisses me gently before disappearing.

"Where is this, and why did you bring me here?" I ask Dabriel, and I watch as he steps back and pulls his shirt off. I didn't see the slits before; they are down the sides of his shirt, and they come apart when he pulls. It makes it easy for the shirt to come off. I'm about to comment about how cool that is when I see his chest. Men's chests can be works of art, but Dabriel's is something else.

He has hard pecs that lead to an eight pack that dips to his white trousers. There is also a long scar across his chest, it's pale and looks old. I wonder how that happened.

He undoes the top button on his trousers as I watch, and he turns around. My eyes widen when I see his firm ass as his trousers fall to the ground. He kicks them off with his shoes and jumps into the pool with one long dive. I move away when the water splashes me, but I come back close to the edge as he rises in the middle of the pool. His white hair comes around his shoulders as the band is loosened, and his wings are spread out, dripping sparkling water.

"The reason I brought you here is because this is my favourite place, and it's mine. Growing up, I was alone a lot. I had a lot of pressure on me at a young age, and I hated that," he tells me. I watch in wonder as white symbols appear all over his body, there isn't a space that doesn't have one. They're hard to look at, to see what they are other than the outline shape. They look like a mixture of lines—some are like crosses, and others look like swirls. I wonder what they mean.

"My mother went into early labour. I wasn't expected for a month, and she was out in the human world. She was helping a young, human child with cancer and had just healed him. She had me in a park in the middle of Indiana, and she didn't survive it. Angel births are difficult, and mothers rarely survive," he says gently.

"I'm so sorry," I say.

"No one was around, but I started glowing.

Glowing so brightly that the angels couldn't help but come to me. They all had a vision and had to come to me, no matter what, and..." he says.

"They found you," I finish his sentence.

"Yes, and my body was covered in white symbols as my dead mother held onto me. My father never truly cared for her. The bastard had gotten someone else pregnant, while my mother was still pregnant with me. I knew he never cared for my mother growing up, but I learnt how much he despised me with every glance he gave me. I don't remember him much as he died when I was very young, but what I do remember is being ignored," he says and takes a breath.

"The angels took me home, and when the news came that the other princes were born, they worshipped me: the prince that was so strong that the goddess had sent him. Then my two younger brothers were born, and my father was devoted to them. I think I threatened his power even as a baby," he says.

"Do your people like your brothers like your father did?" I ask.

"Yes. They are cruel and don't hesitate in killing someone," Dabriel says, his symbols glowing brighter. "I always let my opponent go. I won't kill without reason, or prove myself to anyone," Dabriel says softly. I just nod.

"You don't have to prove yourself to anyone because of a prophecy. What happened was not your fault, and what we do in our future is up to us," he tells me.

"Still, many people have died," I say, thinking of Paris. I was there with Atti and Dabriel recently, enjoying Disneyland with all the other normal people. I wonder what's left of the place where I shared my first kiss with Atti.

"And many more will, that is just the way things are. But if we fight–if you fight–we can make a future worth living in," he says.

"Together?" I ask him.

"Yes, because I love you, Winter. I will love you until I take my last breath and even after my life ends," Dabriel says, and my breath catches.

I don't say anything as I pull my shirt off. I slowly take all my clothes off as he watches me. Both of us are silent, and he swims close to the edge in front of me. When all my clothes are gone, I sit down on the edge, and his warm hands go to my hips. He lifts me into the warm water, our bodies pressed together and our lips seconds apart.

"Cor meum tibi, quod tuum est meum in

sempiternum," he whispers. Before I can ask what he means, he kisses me. My back is pushed carefully against the pool wall as I hook my legs around his waist. Dabriel takes his time, stroking my body with his hands until I can't think straight. When I stroke him and guide him inside me, he starts glowing brighter. White symbols cover every part of his body as he pushes himself fully inside me. He kisses my lips before grabbing hold of my hips and drawing out every thrust, making me scream out in pleasure with every movement. He glows so brightly, all I can see is white.

"Dabriel, I love you," I whisper again and again as we both find our finish. A slight burning fills the middle of the top of my back where my shoulder blades meet making me wince.

"My mark," Dabriel says and kisses my forehead. He pulls me lower in the pool until the water stops the burning.

"That feels great," I say, and he laughs.

"I hope so, my little wildfire."

"Why do you call me that?" I ask him.

"Because you have the power to destroy everything in your path. Even if it's taking their hearts or making them bow to you. It's who you are, you stole every part of me from the first moment we met," he says. I don't know how he does it, but his words make me fall in love with him a little bit more.

"When you took my seat in the restaurant," I mumble.

He laughs, "Yes."

"What were the words you said to me? I didn't recognise the language," I mumble. I also wonder what the new mark looks like.

"The ancient mating words in Latin," Dabriel says and kisses me before he tells me the sweetest and truest words he has ever said to me.

"My heart is yours forever."

CHAPTER 21

JAXSON

"Freddy, turn that music down!" I shout across the hall of the castle. Freddy's room is at the very end of the corridor which has the guys' rooms and Winter's in the middle. I want him close to us.

"He is acting like a teenager already," Wyatt says, coming to stand next to me.

"I'm just glad Anna has taken Marie to visit her parents for the day on the other side of the castle," I tell him. I did offer Anna a room in this corridor, but she decided to stay in the block of rooms the wolves are taking over. She says it's nice to have the help all the time. Marie looks so much like Fergus, it's haunting. I wish I could have saved him.

"Winter is coming soon," Wyatt replies, and I

nod, swallowing my grief at both my brother and sister being gone.

"She has mated to Dabriel," I tell Wyatt. I'm not surprised he felt the change, too, yesterday. I felt when she mated to Wyatt as well. It's like Winter is a link between us all. There has always been a link, a reason we all got along, but it's stronger now. I would die for any of them, to protect them.

"So, you think I should tell him?" Wyatt asks me. I know what he's referring to.

"Yes. We both had shit fathers. Freddy deserves to know he has a good fucking one," I say, and Wyatt pats me on the shoulder.

"Thank you. Come train with me. I've missed kicking your ass," he says, and I laugh.

"I could do with some sword training," I say and walk out the door. We go to the training room, which is outside the castle and actually just a huge room inside a stone building. The room is full of wolves and a few vampires. None of them are fighting together, and there's a clear divide. Every one of them bows when they see us both. At least they do that together. The amount of fucking fights we've had is unreal. I know they hate each other, but all of them are hiding here. Many of the wolves look at Wyatt with distrust. I feel their worry in my bond, and I try to send calm to them.

"A fight between the vampire king and wolf king. Should be interesting to watch," I shout, and a few wolves cheer. The vampires stop what they are doing to watch. I grab two heavy swords and chuck one at Wyatt, who catches it perfectly. The wolves move away to make a large circle in the middle of the room. I stand a distance away from Wyatt and hold my sword up.

"Come on then, vampire," I grin, and he laughs before he charges with his own sword. I swerve to avoid him and swing around, but he is as quick as I am, and he meets my swing.

We fight for ages, neither one of us giving up and both of us dripping with sweat.

"Hey," Winter says, making me turn, and I feel the sword pressed against my neck a second later.

"Unfair distraction," I say.

"Never be distracted," Wyatt shrugs and drops his sword.

"Fucker," I mutter and walk over to Winter who smiles.

"Did Atti bring you?" I ask as I kiss her.

"Yes, and Milo came too, but he went to hang out with Freddy," she says. She treats Milo like her own child and not a mini-demon. I'm thankful Milo is nothing like the rest of his alcoholic kind, but it's still strange how well-trained she has him. They are way too alike; both of them eat my food and adore chocolate.

"Hey, sweetheart," Wyatt says as he comes over, and he leans down to kiss her. I always hated the idea of sharing her. Fucking hated it, but I don't anymore. It seems right.

"Hey, how's everything going?" she asks us both.

"Good, the castle isn't far from being done, and the wolves are settling a little better with the vampires. Freddy and his friend Mich have made friends with a vampire child their age. It's a start," I tell her. Wyatt seems to like this information as he smirks a little.

"That's great," she grins.

"I have a present for Freddy," she holds up a paper bag.

"Let's go then," I say and link my hand with hers. Wyatt walks behind us as we go to the castle. The few wolves we cross bow to us, the vampires do the same. The music is still loud outside Freddy's room, and I knock loudly.

"A girl is about to come into that mess of a

room you call a bedroom."

I hear the music being turned off before Freddy opens the door. His hair is all over the place, and his crinkled clothes are the same he slept in.

"Hey, Winter," his little face lights up.

"I got you something, can I come in?" she asks, and he opens the door. It's not too bad, but I still have to pick some clothes off the floor and bed. I chuck them in the basket by the door and close it. Wyatt leans on the wall by the dresser, and Freddy glares at him.

Winter sits on the end of his bed, and Milo flies over to her shoulder as Freddy sits next to her and opens the bag.

"Wow, it's a wand," Freddy holds it up.

"It's made from a witch stone. It's a spirit wand, I thought it looked Harry Potter-like," Winter says, and he nods. The wand starts glowing and Winter tries to pull it out of his hand as Freddy's eyes roll back, going fully white.

"Freddy!" Winter shouts. I rush in front of him and hold his head in my hands, but he doesn't respond. Wyatt pulls the wand with Winter, but it's stuck in his grip, and I shake his head a little.

"Freddy!" I shout, holding his chin up, and he finally snaps out of it. The wand stops glowing, and

Freddy lets it fall to the ground. Standing, Freddy pulls away from me.

"You're my father," Freddy says with a glare at Wyatt. Wyatt backs up a little, but doesn't take his eyes off Freddy. Fucking hell, what did the light-up stick tell him? How the hell did it tell him that?

"Yes," Wyatt answers simply.

"You didn't tell me?" Freddy looks at me with anger and a slight bit of fear. I can't tell him being a half wolf and half vampire is safe—I have no idea what he will become when he gets older. When wolves are around sixteen, they go through a change. Their wolves change size, some are smaller, but most become bigger. This is also the time they get extra abilities. Freddy already has a few: fast healing, immunity to silver, and he is so fast for his age.

"I was sworn not to tell you by your mother, she didn't want you to know until she could tell you, but that didn't happen. After that, it was safer for you not to know. I wanted you to have the most normal upbringing I could give you," I tell him. His brown eyes, so much like Demi's, watch me. The boy has already been through so much at such a young age. I really didn't give him that much of a fucking normal upbringing like I wanted to.

"How did you know?" I ask him, and Freddy stands up.

"That wand showed me my mother. She was standing right next to me, and she told me who he is to me. She said she loved me and loved you," Freddy points at Wyatt. Winter looks down, and Wyatt's jaw is ticking as he watches Freddy.

"You saw Demi's ghost?" Wyatt asks, a hint of the love in his voice he had for my sister. I glance at Winter, but she doesn't seem to be upset about it. If anything, she just looks worried as she glances between Freddy and Wyatt.

Freddy starts shaking, his whole body getting close to shifting in anger.

"Freddy, listen to me," I say, adding a little alpha power, and I draw his gaze away from Wyatt.

"This changes nothing. I'm still here for you, and so is Winter. Wyatt is your father and a good man; one of the best men I know, and I would trust him with my life. I grew up with Wyatt; he might be a stubborn little git, but he is my brother. Give him a chance. I'm not telling as your alpha or commanding you. I'm asking as your uncle and your friend," I say. Freddy looks at Wyatt for a long time, the stubbornness in his jaw reminds me of his dad.

"Tell me about my mother and you," Freddy says as the shaking stops, and he looks calm. I see Wyatt nod from the corner of my eye. Winter gives me a relieved look, and I smile. Fucking hell, that could have gone badly.

"Let's go for a walk, Freddy," Wyatt says, and he opens the door. He doesn't wait as he walks out, but he glances at Winter. I see her nod at him before he turns.

Freddy follows but stops in front of me and asks, "Wyatt brought my mum to you, didn't he?"

"Yes, and he stayed to protect her. Even after she died, he stayed around and protected the pack. Even you."

"Okay," Freddy says, and he hugs me. I wrap my arms around him, remembering the late nights where he would wake up crying from his fear of lightning as a baby, and the first time we played basketball together. I knew he was never mine, but I treated him like he was. He has always been more than my nephew to me; he is a son to me. Freddy lets go and walks out.

"Smart boy," Winter comments, watching the doorway. She sits on the end of Freddy's bed and picks the wand up.

"Atti put some magic into it. He said it would just shoot white sparks," Winter admits.

"I'll have a word about giving real magic toys to a kid later," I say with a groan. I should have known Atti would have something to do with this.

"Sorry, Wolfman, I should have—" she starts.

I wave a hand to cut her off. "I know. Don't worry. No harm was really done, but Atti is a strong enough witch to know what magic he is fucking with," I say and sit by her on the bed.

"Family good," Milo says making Winter jump. Even I forgot the little shit was here.

"Do you have family, Milo?" Winter asks him as he flies into her hand in her lap.

"Yes, but like drink," he says sadly. Winter and Alex have been working on his speech. It isn't great, but I doubt he had much time to learn when he was with the others. Massive parties where they wreck shit aren't good for learning. I didn't know they could speak more than two words before I met Milo.

"Why don't you drink and party like them?" I ask him, and he turns to look at me. I don't know how he managed to get the weird, pink, tutu dress thing he is wearing, but fuck, he looks weird. I thought he was a guy?

"We used to be different," he says, and I nod.

"You know you're family to me now, Milo," Winter says, and Milo flies to her cheek, he presses a little kiss to her.

"Same," he says, and Winter's whole face lights up. The little thing may be annoying, but if he can make Winter happy then, fuck it, we're keeping him.

"If you stay away from my fucking chocolate brownies and don't make a bed out of them, I'll keep you around," I say, and Winter snorts in laughter.

"They nice, and I eat bed," Milo shrugs.

That little fucker.

"Can't be as bad as the bowl he filled with Atti's chocolate milkshake and lay in it naked. Atti said he would never get the image out of his head," Winter tells me.

"Yummy," Milo says, and I laugh.

"I've changed my mind, I like him," I say, and Winter grins.

"How long did you know my mother for?" Freddy asks me. My son is looking at me like he's seeing me for the first time. In a way, he is. This is fucked up, and yet, I'm glad he knows. I felt like a weird stalker following him around the castle. I did learn that he is strong and good with a sword but fights like Jaxson. I can fix that. I know he's smart, smarter than others seem to realise.

"I knew Demi my whole life. I remember her always being around. Her human foster mother was my maid, and she brought Demi with her to learn how to clean," I tell Freddy. We stop talking when he sees a bench and sits down. I sit next to him and just look at him. He looks like me a little, but so much like Demi.

"So, she was your slave," Freddy deduces.

"For a time, but, honestly, she was the worst one and just told me point-blank to get over myself. Demi was real when the rest of my people were not. Most people were scared of me or wanted to get close because I would be king. Demi just wanted a friend, and that's what we were at the start," I tell him. When he doesn't respond, I keep talking.

"Then things changed one night. After that, we kept our relationship a secret. We didn't have a choice, and I wanted to get her out."

"Why didn't you just run away with her?" Freddy asks me.

"Part of me–back then–loved my father, and I didn't want to run away. I loved Demi, but she wouldn't ask me to do that," I say. It's true, I used to look up to him. I'm not sure why I did, but when he had Demi killed, that ended any good feelings I had for him.

"Two months later, my father bragged about how he had the half-sister to the werewolf prince. I knew he meant Demi because she was the only wolf in the castle. I took her to Jaxson the next day. She wanted me to stay, but I knew we could never work.

It was better for her to have Jaxson look after her and find a wolf to have a life with," I say.

"So you walked away?" Freddy growls out.

"No. I stayed in town. I stayed close, because I couldn't walk away," I tell him, and he doesn't look at me.

"Where were you when she died?" he asks and looks over at the castle.

"My father planned it all. He called me back to the castle, said it was urgent, and I was needed. I shouldn't have gone," I admit to him, it was a stupid move.

"Why did you fall in love with my mother, when you knew Winter would come into your life?" Freddy asks, seeming older than he is.

"Falling in love is never a choice. It's something that takes over you and knocks you on your ass when you least expect it. It happened to me, both with Demi and Winter. Just because I'm with Winter, I haven't forgotten your mum," I tell him and place my hand on his shoulder. It's the first time he has let me touch him, and I know it's a big step when he doesn't move.

"I wish I remembered her," he says sadly.

"I always wish the same with my mother, too. I never had anyone around to tell what she was really like, only rumours. You have that with me; I will tell you anything you want about Demi," I say, and he looks over at me. One nod, and then he stands up, and I move my hand away.

"Jaxson is a dad to me. Don't expect me to start calling you dad, I don't even call him that," Freddy warns, making me smirk.

"No problem, son," I lean back on the bench.

"You can't call me that," Freddy says, and he crosses his arms and looks at me like he wants to kill me. There's my son.

"I'll do whatever I want, and you *are* my son. If you don't want to call me dad, that's fine, but I am going to be a dad to you," I tell him honestly. I'm not hiding him anymore; people are going to know that half-breeds exist, and that Freddy is my heir. That makes him a prince, whether he likes it or not.

"I don't want that," he says angrily, his whole body shaking with anger.

"I know," I reply, and I watch as he storms off.

Drake and Alex walk over to me, coming out of the trees near the edge of the castle. Alex still has twigs in her hair, and Drake has a big grin as he kisses her. Both of them are dressed for training, the camp we have set up is on the other side of the castle. It's good for the werewolves and vampires to train together. Not that they do, but it's progress that they aren't trying to kill each other.

"I figured out what's in Paris," Drake says as he stops in front of me, his voice going stern and losing whatever happiness he had with Alex mere seconds ago. She clings onto his arm, and I have a feeling it's not going to be a good answer.

"Well?" I ask.

"Silver weapons. The biggest collection in the world is on display in a museum in Paris. He wants the people and the weapons," Alex says, her voice high and panicked.

"That's fucking perfect," I grit out. I stand up and run my fingers through my hair as I pace. How can we tell our people and Winter about this?

"There's another thing we need to tell you about," Alex adds in, and I turn to meet her eyes, but it's Drake that replies.

"Humans are posting online about groups of demons walking around. They are always in groups of ten. Some are recognising them as the missing people that are in Paris. The government is struggling to keep this a secret."

"Most of the humans just think they are strange people wearing odd makeup, but I looked at the videos on YouTube. They are demons, and the groups are everywhere. Not attacking, just walking from town to town. They don't respond when people talk to them, they just keep walking–" Alex says.

"He's sending out patrols to find us," I cut her off. It's smart.

"Why? Winter said he has been at this castle. He killed Elissa here, so he knows where we are," Alex says, reminding me of Winter's dream.

"Maybe it's hidden from him, I'm not sure," I say.

"We need to be sure. We have so many young here," Alex says.

I nod at her. "I am well aware of our issues, but don't tell Winter about this. Not until she wins these fights. She doesn't need any more worry," I say, and they both nod in agreement. "Go and have the day off. I will train the men and women today," I say.

They both look happy at the idea. Drake picks Alex up and throws her over his shoulder as she squeals. "Thank you, prince," Drake chuckles when Alex tries to wriggle free.

I want that peace with Winter one day. Hopefully, one day soon.

CHAPTER 23

"Wow," Atti says, and then clears his throat as he looks at me. I should be the one saying "wow" when Atti is dressed like a hot pirate. He has a loose white shirt on that dips to show off his impressive chest. He has a white cloak on, stretched around his large shoulders and tight black trousers. Honestly, I expect him to throw me over his shoulder and take me to his ship.

"This looks okay?" I ask, glancing down at the white, lacy dress I'm wearing. Tonight is the summer solstice, and witches all go to the trees to dance and celebrate. Atti wants to take me; Leigha is watching the house, and Dabriel had to visit the pack to heal a few people after a fight broke out.

The wolves and vampires are still having trouble mixing. I was left to Alex and her fashion do over.

"You look amazing, no hot, no wait, I can think of a good word," he mumbles out, making me chuckle.

"So, what happens tonight?" I ask him.

"A big party and..." Atti stops and shakes his head. He takes my hand and pulls me close, "I'd rather just show you," he says, and we float away with his power.

When we reappear, we are in the middle of a crowd. A few people stare at us and bow their heads. Other witches look on in worry or just walk away from us. It takes me a second to recognise them as witches because they all have their hoods down. Most of them have black or dark-blonde hair like Atti. There are a few with silver hair, which makes me wonder which side they are from. They have a mix of skin tones as well, but most have a gold complexion like Atti's. Sun-kissed skin. I glance up at the stars in the sky; they are so bright here.

There's a long table full of different food spread down the middle of the trees. Children and parents spin in circles as music plays fast, merry tunes.

The trees have yellow bunting hanging between

them, and I can hear the trees singing to the music. They're happy.

I smile up at Atti who takes my hand and leads me through the crowd to the dancers. He spins us around, and we hold hands as we dance around in circles like the others. I laugh as he pulls me close and spins me out. We dance close, my big smile matching his. Our hips sway to the music, and my head is tucked into his chest.

The song ends, and I clap with everyone else for the small band–just a few witches playing a variety of different instruments with one singer. People are still staring, but it isn't too bad. I kind of got used to it at the vampire castle.

"Will you dance with me?" a little girl asks Atti. She looks around five with her white hair in two plaits, and is wearing a little yellow dress. It reminds me of the yellow dress I saw myself wearing as a toddler with my mother. It's hard not to feel the pain with the memory–the tears running down my mother's face.

Her mother, I guess, comes running over and lowers into a bow.

"I am so sorry for my daughter, she doesn't realise who you are," the blonde woman says. She stands up; she has on a simple, white corset dress that falls to the ground.

"I'm just a witch like her. I would love to have this dance with you, my lady," Atti says and does a bow to the girl, who giggles.

Atti holds a hand out, and she takes it. I move back next to the woman and watch as Atti picks the girl up and dances around with her.

"He will make a good father, my lady," the woman says, and I nod watching him. I can't imagine a life where I would feel safe enough to have a baby. The world we live in isn't safe, and yet, I could see a little girl with my hair and maybe Atti's eyes. I could imagine having a child with any of my guys.

"Agreed. I'm Winter," I hold out my hand to her, and she accepts it.

"I sincerely hope you win the last fight. I have always believed in the goddess," she tells me. Her light grey eyes are large on her bold-looking face. There's a slight scar by her eye that stands out in her perfect face.

"Thank you," I nod, and she smiles.

"I'm going to try the food; could you tell Atti where I am?" I ask.

"Of course, my lady," she bows again, and I move away towards the food.

"This is a message from the queen," a woman I recognise steps in front of me. The woman is one of the two I usually see with the queen. She is the pretty one, with the long blonde hair, and is a light witch. I wonder why she is on Taliana's side and not Atti's.

"What is it?" I ask, and she smirks before answering.

"The next fight is the last, and you are allowed two women to fight with you. This fight will be the end, the queen is done with the games as we have a war to fight," she says, her voice echoing, and everyone stops to stare at us. The music cuts off a second before I feel Atti appear next to me and slip his hand around my waist.

"Fine," I reply. The woman disappears. The witches all go back to whatever they were doing, but a lot of them are still watching us.

"Who are you choosing?" Atti immediately asks me.

"Leigha and Alex. I don't know any others to help me," I say.

"Two vampires are not a good idea. Leigha, yes, but Alex is still so untrained," he says. I guess he is right; Alex wouldn't be a good choice. Also, I would be way too distracted trying to protect her.

"Who would you suggest?" I ask.

"Katy or maybe Lucinda," he tells me. I didn't realise he knew her.

"Why?"

"They are both strong, and Jaxson has made Katy a guard. Lucinda is an alpha of strong blood. I believe one of them would be the ideal person to have at your side."

"I will ask Jaxson. She's only sixteen, and Lucinda has a lot of responsibilities," I say.

"And you are only twenty. Age is just a number for us, we don't have the pleasure of being innocent for so long. Our children don't know a time without death and war," Atti says, his eyes watching the dancers.

"Twenty-one in two months," I say, and Atti smiles.

"We will have to celebrate," he winks.

"Only if the whole world isn't destroyed, you mean," I joke a little too loudly. Several people look my way. Okay, maybe a bad joke.

"I'm going to feed you so you stop talking. I have better ways to keep you quiet, but we can't do those in public," Atti winks at me again, and I laugh with warm cheeks. He walks us closer to the table of food, his arm tight around my waist.

"Oh, chocolate cake!" I point at a large chocolate cake, and he walks us over. He cuts me a big piece and then gets me a fork.

"I would try the whole romantic feeding you thing, but I'm honestly scared you would try to eat me and not in the good way," he laughs.

"What's the good way?" I innocently ask him, and he smirks.

"The same good way I would enjoy eating you," he winks, and I blush, my mouth closed around a piece of chocolate cake.

"And, baby," Atti says as he moves his head close to my ear, "I can be as slow or fast as you like," he whispers. I nearly choke on my chocolate cake at his seductive words. I was wrong; fucking hell, Atti can flirt like the best of them. I miss this side to Atti, the less serious side.

"What was it like growing up around here?" I ask him as we eat.

"I didn't get out much. My mother was protective, to say the least; she couldn't cope with me being far from her until I was stronger and able to protect myself," he says.

"So, you were lonely?" I ask.

"No, just bored. You forget I used to sneak out and see the others. When I first started seeing Wyatt, he was an angry kid. It was fun to wind him up. We both came up with this great idea to see the other princes. Jax was cool, but Dabriel tried to kill us. He was a serious one with a stick up his butt," Atti says, and I laugh at his choice of words.

"Anyway, my mother finally caught on about my disappearing acts. Witches usually can't use the power to move until they hit sixteen, so she didn't know I could do it. She showed me the castle and told me it was safe to play there." His words are tinted in sadness. "The rest of my childhood was council meetings, fighting in the arena, and learning everything I could about ruling," he tells me.

"You will make a good king," I say.

He looks down at me. "With you at my side, I will," he whispers and kisses me. "You had a little chocolate on your lips," he smirks.

"You don't need an excuse to kiss me, Atti," I grin.

"I know," he smiles and wraps an arm around me. We both watch the dancers for a while, lost in our thoughts.

"Here, my lady, I brought you a drink. They're made from the grapes I grew in my garden," a woman says with long, black hair as she stops in front of us; a dark witch. She hands Atti and me two glasses.

"Thank you," I say and drink some as she moves into the crowd. The grape juice is soft and sweet. It's really nice.

I eat a few more bites of cake before I start feeling hot.

"Winter," I hear, and I try to respond, but nothing comes out.

CHAPTER 24

ATTICUS

"Dabriel," I shout as I hold Winter to my chest, while I pull on my magic to find him. I reappear just inches away from him.

"What happened?" Dabriel instantly asks as he takes Winter from me. She isn't awake, and she's barely breathing. I don't feel myself move as I watch Dabriel glow white all over to the point that I can't see Winter anymore. I don't look at anything other than the light. I feel Jaxson move next to me and put his hand on my shoulder, but I don't respond. What feels like years later, but is probably only moments, Dabriel dials down the glowing, so I can see Winter. She looks pale and is still sleeping, but Dabriel nods. That nod is all I need, and I rest my hands on my knees as I take a deep breath.

Jaxson goes over and strokes Winter's hair away from her eyes.

"What the fucking hell happened to her, and why isn't she awake?" Jaxson snaps as he faces me.

"A witch gave her a drink, it was poisoned," I say as I straighten up. I thought I'd fucking lost her; I can't lose her. Winter means everything to me.

"D, why isn't she awake?" I ask, but the door slamming open again behind makes me turn to look. I notice for the first time that we are in the castle, in the kitchens. Dabriel was cooking when I came here, I realize as I spot the stuff on the sides. Wyatt, with Milo on his shoulder, storms into the room.

"Oreos?" Milo asks as he flies towards the cupboards. Wyatt storms over to us, his eyes completely silver in anger and leans over Winter when Jaxson moves out the way.

"Why is she sleeping?" he asks.

"She is–" Dabriel starts, but Milo interrupts as he chews on an Oreo.

"Dream-calling," he muffles out.

"Again?" Wyatt asks sharply. None of us reply.

"I'll take Winter back to her room, we will wait for her to wake up," Dabriel suggests. We nod, and he walks out with her. I clench my fists, cracking my knuckles as I look at my friends.

"We have a witch to find, and I know exactly where to find her," I say. Words are not needed as Wyatt and Jax put their hands on my shoulders. I move us to my city, straight into the castle. The guards rush forward, and I raise my arm, using my air power to swipe them across the hallway, and they slam into the wall.

"No fun," Wyatt smirks. I walk forward and slam the door to my mother's old room open. I don't expect it to be empty and completely ruined. Someone has set the place on fire; the windows are smashed, and there's nothing left. I can only hope her familiar was buried. Familiars die with us, their lives linked to ours. I have to ignore the painful lump in my throat as I look at the room my mother loved. It increases my anger as I walk out of the room and down the corridor. The next two guards we come across rush at us when they should be running away. Two female dark witches call on fire and try to throw it at us. I blow it away with my air and hold the two witches in the air. Their hoods fall back as they try to escape.

"Where the fuck is Taliana?" I shout. Neither answers, loyal to their fake queen. I'm about to try different, harsher actions to get an answer when the bitch in question walks in.

"If you wanted time alone with me, you only had to ask, Atticus," she purrs out.

"Not even in your dreams, Taliana," I sneer and drop the witches. I stalk over to her and stand inches away as I speak.

"Where is the witch who poisoned Winter tonight?" I shout.

"I do not know who you are talking of. I swore not to hurt her," she smiles, a seductive tone in her voice as she moves closer. The scent of whatever perfume she's wearing hits me and makes me feel sick. She makes me feel sick.

"Let's go and discuss this privately. I can make you much happier than the human ever will," she suggests and goes to place her hand on my chest.

"Do you think I would ever look twice at you? You killed my mother, and I am in love with a woman who is a million times fucking better than you. Find the witch who attacked her, or I swear I will kill you and anyone that gets in my way. I am not playing fucking games anymore," I say, and I grab her hand to push her away.

"Fine, the witch is dead. I didn't kill her, but someone else did. They used demon powers, destroying her home. I believe she was killed moments after she returned home," Taliana says.

"I want to see," I demand.

"I will take you," she holds out a hand.

"No, just the address. I know my city like the back of my hand," I say, and her face tightens in anger. I'm glad I'm finally pissing her off.

"Fine, but you will be mine, Atticus," she says and tells me the address. I walk back to Jaxson and Wyatt who nod, clearly hearing all of the conversation. My brothers always have my back.

"How did you kill my mother? Dabriel couldn't heal her," I say and look back to meet her cold eyes.

"Injuries from demon-touched weapons can't be healed, and I will kill Winter with one as well," she says, and Jaxson's growl fills the room. Dabriel starts glowing brightly, and I debate whether it's worth killing her.

"I will enjoy watching my queen kill you," I say and call on my power to get us out of here.

I move us to the street that Taliana said. It's close to my own home, and we walk down the quiet street until we find the home we need. A few witches in light hoods bow as we walk past. When we get to number seven, the house where the witch lived, it's easy to see the evil that's happened here. I wonder what Dabriel would see when he looks at a demon and reads their aura.

I walk in, as the door is open, and the wards are down. The living room is destroyed, blood covering the walls and floors. Crystal powder is all over the floor, what a waste.

"I smell the witch's blood and a demon," Jaxson says.

"Why would a demon do this?" Wyatt asks as he looks around the room in disgust.

"How did they get in the city is another important question," I say.

"The witch is dead; she would have had an easier death if we found her first. She clearly suffered," Jaxson gestures around the room. I take one more look at the room before we leave. Jaxson is right; there is nothing we can do here anymore.

As soon as Winter wakes up, we will plan a way to make the city safe.

CHAPTER 25

"*Have you come to make a promise?*" *a sweet voice asks. The voice is familiar, and I struggle to open my eyes. My body feels tired, and I'm not sure why. When I see the purple trees and look down at my feet in the yellow grass, I know why I'm tired.*

Shoot, I've dream-called the fairy again. I turn slightly to see her standing at the line of trees a few feet away.

Lily stands looking over at me, in a black dress with a cut-out in the middle. She isn't wearing a cloak today, so I can see how she has a perfect body to go with her beauty. All supernaturals have this perfect-looking thing sorted.

Her long, strawberry-blonde hair flutters in the warm breeze. The air even smells nice here; it tastes like sweets as I breathe it in.

"For your help?" I ask, turning to fully face her, and I go

to take a step forward, but I can't move. I brush my hands down the white dress I'm wearing and look at her.

"The demon king will demand the world, and only I can help you. What I ask for in return isn't terrible," she says with a slight giggle.

"So, explain exactly what the offer is," I say. I can't say we don't need the help. I saw first-hand how weapons are useless, and it took two wolves to take down one of them. The witches' powers aren't going to be useful against demons unless they have weapons that work. The vampires could team up, but we don't have the numbers anymore. There just aren't enough of us if he has turned even a quarter of Paris. That doesn't even include the vampires and humans that were in the castle. The angels won't help, not unless they're sure they'll win. Well, that's what Dabriel thinks. The dark angels' power to cause pain when they touch someone won't help kill the demons when they look like emotionless zombies. We don't have a big enough army with the low birth rate and numerous deaths that have happened because of the wars between the supernatural people. The witches and angels fought for years and killed each other. Then, the werewolves and vampires declared war and did the same. This is the most vulnerable time for them, for us all, and we now have the biggest threat on our doorstep. The demons can't be killed by silver, but we can.

"I offer you this for a single promise. I swear to send five

thousand of my Fray army to your world. They will carry four weapons each, and you may keep three of their weapons for your own men and women. When the war is won, they will all leave and not come back," she says.

"How will they get here?" I ask.

"The war will happen on the Winter solstice, we can travel through the dimensions on that day only. The earth is weak on that day, and that's why the demon king needs to use it."

"What will you ask in return?" I ask her, crossing my arms, and she smiles.

"In your world, there is a half Fray child. I wish for you to send her to me when you meet her," she smiles.

"How do you know I will?" I ask.

"Your mother told me," she says, and I look away. I don't know why it bothers me that she had such a good relationship with my mother. I guess I could almost be jealous that I didn't get that time with her.

"How would I send the child back?" I ask.

"When you make the promise, you will only have to touch her, and the portal will open. Ancient magic will take her to me," she says.

"Why can't you just find her?" I ask.

"I can't risk being in your world long, my soldiers will only stay a day to win the war. Fray do not belong in the human world, and half children are rare gifts," she tells me.

"Do you believe in the goddesses?" I ask.

"Not yours. We have our own," she replies, she looks up to the sky and then lowers her creepy, yellow eyes on me.

"Why do you want the child?" I ask. I can't send any child to someone if they plan to hurt her. Not that I have a clue if Lily is lying to me as she replies.

"She is royalty. There is little of the Royal Fray left," she answers. I watch her closely, but she looks like she's being honest. I feel my back warming up, like it's burning.

"Make the promise, your mates are calling," she says.

"I promise," I say, and feel a snap around my wrists like shackles. When I look at my wrists, there are two white lilies in the middle of both of them.

"I promise my side. Thank you, queen Winter," she says.

"You never told me your full name."

"Queen Lily. Queen of all the Fray," she says, and my eyes widen. She is a queen here.

"One more thing, queen Winter, the portal to the demon dimension must be closed with the king on the other side. The only way to close it is a death. Not just any death, only one with goddess's blood may close the portal. I am truly sorry." She lowers her head to me. Does that mean I will have to die?

"No," I shake my head; no one can die to close the portal anyway, it's in the middle of the vampire castle. How would I even get close enough?

"Her saviour will die when the choice is made," Lily says gently as I feel myself falling.

I blink my eyes as I open them, I'm lying on top of Atti, and he's gently snoring.

"Atti," I whisper, wondering how long I fell asleep for this time. The last time was two weeks. Lily's final words come rushing back to me. The prophecy said my saviour would die and someone has to die to close the portal. Only I have goddess blood, so surely, I would die?

Who the hell is my saviour?

In a way, I've been saved by a lot of people I care about. I won't let any of them die for me, no way in hell. I'll send my grandfather back to the demon dimension myself and make that choice. It's me that has to pay the price; it was me that opened the portal in the first place. My heart tightens at the thought, but what choice do I have?

"You're awake, thank god," Atti says, and sits up with me. He kisses me gently.

"What the hell is this?" he asks when he sees my wrists. I glance down and see the Lily marks on both my wrists. The dream was real, and it snaps to

G. BAILEY

me what I've done and the choices I have to make in the future.

"I made a promise with the Fray queen. She will send help when we need it. I have to send someone to her, a child that is half Fray. Lily said a portal will open when I touch the child," I tell him. His eyes widen, and he shakes his head.

"I don't know anything about Fray, but how can we know to trust a promise from her?" he asks.

"You shouldn't make a promise with Fray," Jaxson says, coming into the room. He sits next to Atti and me. I turn slightly to look at him as he takes my hand in his warm one.

"What do you mean?" I ask.

"I don't know, lass, but Lucinda talks to plants remember?" he asks, and I nod. I once saw Lucinda on pack lands, with both her hands on a tree, and she was glowing slightly yellow. Jaxson was with me and explained about her power to talk to trees and most plants. I was shocked that they spoke at all. I know, after everything I've seen, I shouldn't be shocked, but I was. It was only a few weeks later that the jewel trees sang with me. Weird shit happens.

"I told her you had been dream-calling a Fray, and that's what the plants told her when she asked them for me. Not to make a promise with a Fray," he says, and a cold sweat fills me. That can't be a good sign. Why do I feel like I've just made a huge mistake?

"I made one with the queen," I say quietly. Jaxson looks up at the ceiling, his jaw ticking and his grip on my hand tightens.

"We will work it out," Jaxson finally says.

"The last fight is today," Atti says.

"I don't even remember going to bed, we were dancing at the summer solstice and then . . ." I drift off when I realise I don't have a clue what happened. I vaguely remember the queen's friend speaking to me about the fight, and then that's it.

"Then you were poisoned," Jaxson finishes, and I can't remember it. Is that why I feel so tired? I felt tired before I went to fairyland, but now, every part of my body is aching like I've been working out with Leigha for a week.

"The grape juice had poison in it, only yours. Dabriel saved you," Atti says. His voice is tense and full of anger. I bet the guys had to stop him from killing someone for poisoning me.

"Where is he, so I can thank him?" I ask.

"With Wyatt at the castle. A few vampires were attacked last night by demons in the next town.

They just walked into the bar and went straight for them. The humans ran away, and there were only ten demons, but everyone has been called to the castle. Dabriel needs to heal them. They lost five vampires. Only three survived and just barely. They said the demons were too strong," Jaxson says, and I know why I feel so worried and sad. I'm picking up on Wyatt's emotions even from this distance away.

"Oh no," I say quietly.

"You need to eat and get ready; I'm here to be a snack. I'm the only one you haven't fed on, and you need any help you can get in the fight," Atti says.

Jaxson stands. "I'll get you some normal food, too. Have fun," he smirks at my shocked face and walks out.

"You sure?" I ask as I look at Atti, and he laughs. Atti pulls me onto his lap and turns his head to the side.

"Are you kidding me? I've been fucking waiting for this for months," he says, and I laugh. My laughter drifts off as I smell him. He smells so sweet, and I'm powerless to stop myself as I bite into his neck. He tastes better than anything I could think of, and he groans, pulling me closer with every second. I moan when Atti's hand slides down my stomach and even lower to my core, as I feed on him. The pressure is crazy, and I let him take me over the edge as he slowly moves his hand against me. When I stop and pull away, he removes his hand and smiles at me. I wipe the little bit of blood off my lips as he watches. It used to freak me out, drinking blood, but it doesn't anymore.

"Winter, all I want to do is lie you down and make love to you," he says, making me turn bright red. I'm such a dork.

"I want that too, I feel incomplete without you," I tell him honestly.

"Soon," he whispers and kisses me.

We eventually leave the bedroom, and I shower. I find my leather outfit and my daggers folded up with a chocolate bar on top of them. That has Alex all over it, and it makes me smile. I decide to plait my hair into the same bun as last time.

When I'm all dressed, I come down the stairs and nearly walk into Jaxson's back when I see Esta by the door.

"What the bloody hell is she doing here?" I ask a little harshly. Esta is dressed to fight, wearing tight black leggings and a short leather top that looks like it's trying to replace her skin. There are guns strapped to her arms and thighs. She also has a large, silver sword on her back. Jaxson told me that a lot of supernaturals don't use guns because the bullets are so small and only a tiny amount of silver. The only good thing is that if you fire enough, it will slow them down and give you time to make a final kill with a sword or something else. Esta doesn't bother looking at me as she speaks.

"I may not like you, my queen, but I have amends to make. Anna is a sister to me and begged me to help you. Katy is too young and Lucinda too old, so here I am; I have the power to move extremely fast, so fast you can't see me. I will help you in the fight, for Anna, but I can't shift. I can't move as fast as a wolf, and it's useless to you anyway," she says, and I turn to look at Jaxson.

"If I could help you I would," he says quickly, and hands me a plate with a sandwich on it. I eat it quickly.

"I don't know, you are a big enough girl to maybe trick the queen into letting you fight," Atti says, and Jaxson turns to glare at him.

"Fucking asshole," Jaxson says, and Atti laughs.

"You have us confused, bro," he says, and I snort a little in laughter. Atti isn't wrong.

Leigha comes into the room, dressed like a leather-loving, warrior princess. Two swords on her back and a load of daggers all over her outfit.

It's a wonder how she doesn't manage to stab herself when she sits down or, hell, just moves.

I would.

"Time to leave," she says, and I look over at Atti. *It's time to win this for him.*

CHAPTER 26

*L*eigha and Esta are standing on either sides of me as we face the empty queen's stand. When we first got here, the crowds of witches were going crazy, screaming my name and Taliana's into the slightly cold air. I glance up just as a few snowflakes fall from the sky.

It's been a long time with us just standing here waiting. Leigha is tapping her foot, and my guys are sending me worried glances. The large, metal gate slowly opens, creaking as it does.

The queen walks out like she hasn't got a care in the world. She is dressed in a long, black dress; it sticks to her small body as she moves and has two massive slits on the side. I guess it's for easy movement. The main difference is that she has the black crown on her head. I haven't seen it since the first day, and its power calls to me. Taliana looks paler than she usually does. I wonder why she doesn't wear the crown all the time. It's so powerful–like Jaxson's and the vampire king's that I've seen. The two witches I usually see with her are at her side, walking close to her under their large cloaks. I haven't discussed it with the guys, but I knew she would fight me. Dabriel couldn't have seen anything, as he would have told the others or me. The guys wouldn't want me fighting her, but this is personal for her. She wants Atti. I'm the only thing in her way of taking Atti and the throne. She will get everything she has ever wanted, and I bet she doesn't want to risk me winning this fight. Taliana stops around five feet in front us, the two witches at her sides undo their cloaks and let them all fall to the ground. I guess it's three against three. At least the odds are fair.

"Let the best queen win," Taliana says, and she flashes straight in front of me. She throws a punch straight into my face, but I'm trained enough to duck. Thank god for my power as a blue wave slams out of me and straight into her. I watch her fly across the stadium and hit the wall hard by the gate.

No one is taking Atti from me.

My hands glow blue as I walk towards her, she stands up and flashes again, this time I don't see her as she appears at my side and slams a kick into my stomach. I fly across the arena and hit my side as I land on the dusty ground.

Air leaves my chest as she raises her hand, and a cold wave of wind pushes into me. I roll onto the ground, dust getting into my mouth and mixing with my blood. I hear a loud scream and turn to see Leigha just as she kills the light witch by shoving a dagger into her throat. I stand up a little shakily as my eyes meet Leigha's, and she drops the witch's body and runs towards me.

"No!" the queen screams in anger and flashes to me again, this time behind me, her hand slides over my mouth as her arm holds me tightly. I feel like I'm drowning, water filling my lungs.

"*Winter,*" Atti shouts in my head, seconds before Taliana's hand is removed, and I fall to the ground. I cough up the water after falling to my knees. I turn to see Leigha fighting with the queen, both of them just as good as the other, as they throw hit after hit.

"Bye, wolfy," I hear near me and snap my head over to see Esta fall to the ground, her stomach ripped open and blood everywhere. Her eyes meet mine, and I know she can't heal from this. An uncontrollable anger fills me when I see the witch standing over her. The dark witch turns to me with a smirk and raises her arms. I pull a dagger out of my belt and rush over. The witch cracks the earth I'm running on, and I see her dark grey eyes glowing. Unfortunately for her, I just jump over the crack and kick her chest as hard as I can as I land. She falls backwards onto the ground. I follow, not feeling my feet on the ground as I walk slowly to her, seeing only my revenge. The fear in her eyes is clear as she watches me.

"My pack," I say, my voice louder than before, and it echoes around the silent arena. I don't think about the witch who pleads for her life as I slam my dagger into her heart. I watch the life leave her eyes before I turn and run to Esta. I pull her head into my lap, and she gazes up at me, blood is pouring out of her mouth. I can hear Leigha fighting with Taliana in the background. I have to give Esta these last moments; no one deserves to die alone.

"Ask the goddess to forgive me," she coughs out. I barely understand her words.

"Why?" I say quietly to her.

"It was me; I killed Fergus and let the vampires in. I wanted them to kill you, and then I would have

Jaxson as my mate. I love him," she says. I watch in shock as she dies in my arms. I'm not sure I know how to give her the forgiveness she wanted now that she is dead. Her blood feels warm against my hands as I hold her, and yet, she feels empty. Anna would hate her for this.

"I forgive you, and your life was payment for that mistake," I say, and look up to catch Jaxson's eyes across the arena. I know he heard every word by the angry look he's giving me. I don't think he's angry with me, but with Esta. I can't believe she did it. I let her body fall gently to the ground and glance over at Leigha as she fights Taliana. *I've had enough.*

I'm covered in blood as I walk over to both of them, my hands glowing, and my power rising. Taliana gets the best of Leigha when she sends a blast of wind at her. Leigha flies across the arena. Taliana flashes to me. Just when she reappears in front of me, I pull for my power. It comes out in a wave as she grabs my arm, this time we both go flying together. She slams into the wall, my body driving hers further into the wall, as her grip on my arm loosens enough for me to pull away.

I wipe the blood off my lip, standing at the same time she does. She smirks before throwing a stream of fire at me. With no time to save myself, and being so close to her, the blue fire consumes me.

"*No!*" I hear Atti scream in my mind. The ground shakes, and I have no doubt that it's Jaxson's power. The fire doesn't hurt my skin; in fact, it feels good.

I walk forward, my clothes burning away as I pull the dagger out of my belt and hold it at my side. The handle is burning hot but doesn't hurt anymore. This must be what I got from Atti. I can't see the queen, but I don't need to. I know she's close to me, I can see her hand. I throw the dagger, and the fire disappears.

The crowd is silent as they watch their dark queen hold a hand over the dagger in her heart.

Taliana dies, my silver eyes reflecting back at me in her own dark ones, and the crown rolls off her head as she falls. I look at her dead body, feeling a little sadness. I didn't want to have to kill her, but there wasn't much choice. *When did I become this person that just killed two people and didn't feel anything doing it?*

I glance over as Atti appears next to me, he wraps his cloak around my naked body, which I'm suddenly very grateful for. I don't know how I forgot

I'm naked. Bloody hell, Alex is going to love this story if I don't tell her the whole part about me nearly getting killed. I glance at Atti, knowing I would do anything for him. I would do anything for any of my men. I reach down and pick the crown up, feeling its power rush over me. That's why Taliana was so powerful; it's the crown.

Atti keeps his hand on my back as I turn in his arms; I lift the crown with both my glowing blue hands.

"My king," I say loudly, and the witches cheer, their support almost deafening through the shouts in our minds and the sound of their clapping hands.

Atti lowers his head, and I put the crown on top. He straightens up and winks at me.

King Atticus Lynx of the witches has finally taken his rightful place.

CHAPTER 27

ATTICUS

"*D*oes it feel weird to be king?" Winter asks as we sit in the high council rooms together. The council rooms take over the entire bottom floor of the castle; it's where all witches can come to have their grievances heard and where we enforce our laws. Our laws are not that different from human ones, and witches rarely break them. The room we are sitting in now has a long, gold table; our seats are in the middle. The rest of the council sits on our sides, four light witches and four dark witches. The room is split like that also, with half the walls white and the other half black. The floor is the same with a gold line in the middle leading up to our seats. The witches have always been divided, but things are changing.

I'll make them. Mags and Jewels were happy to get back to the castle; it's much bigger for them, and they like the massive waterfall in the royal garden. They drink out of it like it's their personal water bowl; it used to drive my mother crazy. The council all stare at us with worry and fear. They all rushed to put together a meeting the second Winter put the crown on my head. The power from the crown floats through me, making me feel like I can do anything with it on my head. It's fucking strong.

What Winter did was crazy, powerful, and a sign of who she really is. I glance down at her as she watches me for a response; she is so lovely. Winter is dressed like a queen today, thanks to her friend's help. She has on a long, white dress, which tightens in the middle and flares out at her sexy hips. Her long, dark-brown hair is straight with just the top part up in some plaits. I know she doesn't even realise it, but she is something else to look at. Every time she walks into a room, she demands attention with her beauty and strength. No matter what happens from today on, she will always be known as a powerful woman. But the prophecy is still bugging me, there's a lot in it that makes little sense.

When I saw her being covered in fire by Taliana, my fucking mind exploded. I tried to flash to her, but Taliana had cast a watertight ward around the arena, and she had two witches keeping it up. I knocked them both out with Jaxson's help and then blasted the ward, but I only got through once Winter had killed Taliana. She must have gotten the power of immunity to fire from me. It's actually a power I have; most witches do. Winter hasn't said much about killing two witches today, she just told me she was okay. I hope the guilt doesn't get to her, but if it does, I'll be at her side. I love her.

"Yes, very weird. I know what my mother warned me about now. The power boost from the crown is strange and a little overwhelming. We need to get you a crown now," I say.

She looks away. "I have one, but I can't, not yet Atti," she says. I get how nervous she is. Putting on this crown is accepting my destiny, which I'm meant to be. I never really thought I'd have to take the throne for many years, my mother's death was not expected. I look around at the familiar faces of the council, the ones who stood at my mother's side for years. It hurts that she isn't at my side to guide me; I'm fucking clueless, but I'm going to do my best for her memory. For Winter.

"In time," I whisper and lift her hand. Her

sparkling, blue eyes lock with mine as I kiss the back of her hand.

"My King and Queen. I wish to thank you for my place on the high council."

The words come from the first male on the witch council in hundreds of years. One of the queen's friends had been a council member, so there was a space when Winter killed her, and I think we need this change.

"It was the right choice," I say, and he lowers his head.

"In fact, I want to show my queen the castle, so goodbye," I say and hold onto Winter's arm as I move us before they say anything. Winter and I have been stuck in meeting after meeting following the fight. The city was out of control, with the dark witches not wanting me on the throne. They are currently locked up until they calm down. Taliana's parents were devastated, which I understand, but I did not condone their decision to try to burn the castle down. Thank god, I was close enough to pull water from the waterfall in the garden and flood that part of the castle. No one was hurt, but I had to lock her parents up. The council believes that they will calm down when things settle down. What we didn't know is how the city has been attacked by demons in the last few weeks. Only groups of ten or so, but they are killing and walking through wards like they aren't there. Thirty witches have been killed in the last two weeks. We have some serious problems, and I've called the witch guard to come here in the morning. The witch guard is a hundred witches who protect our city, and I want to know how they let the demons in. Not one of the witches who died was in the guard. It shouldn't be that way.

"This is my room, well, the one I stay in when I have to be here," I say as we appear in the lounge of the rooms I have. It overlooks the whole city from where we stand; it's similar to the rooms my mother had. They're gone; Taliana destroyed them all. I wish she were alive, so I could fucking kill her again.

"Wow, what a view," Winter says, moving away from me and standing close to the window. She turns her head to look back at me, a small smile on her sweet lips. Winter doesn't even know what she does to me.

"It is," I say, looking only at her. She seems to realise this as she smirks at me.

"I'm surprised you didn't show me your bedroom first," she says with a little wink.

"That's next," I laugh as I walk over to her and

take her head into my hands, and I kiss her. Winter tastes like every sweet you wanted as a child but couldn't have. I move us to my bedroom and rip her clothes off as she pulls my belt open.

I've waited too long for this, for her, and I know she feels the same way.

I love her so much, and I want her to be mine.

When our clothes are gone, I explore every part of her sweet little body with my lips and hands. Loving the little moans she does, and the way she wriggles when I do certain things. I kiss up her soft stomach until we are perfectly aligned.

"I love you, Atti," she whispers as I fill her, and she arches her back. Every part of me demands for my magic to mark her as mine, and I don't hold back as I move inside her, she feels too good. I pull out and roll her onto her knees before entering her again. She seems to understand, or my magic is already affecting her.

She moans as I pick up my pace, and when I know she's close, I rest my hands on her back and push my magic into her. The magic I've never let out, but have always known, blasts around the room as we both scream out each other's names in plea-sure. The mating magic is designed for just one person, and I have always known it, in the back of my mind. It's meant to guide us to who we are meant to be with. Mine always knew it was Winter.

When I can finally open my eyes, Winter is lying on her stomach, her head tilted to look at me with a happy smile. I glance at her back and grin at what I see.

Winter's back is covered in marks. My mark is a tree with large roots. The tree is made of swirls that match the other guys' marks. Winter hasn't seen my mark as it's on my back, but it looks so much better on her. The tree takes over my whole back, but it fits just right on hers.

Jaxson's wolf is near her lovely bottom and there are twirls that rise to join with the phoenix in the middle. The two angel wings are just below her neck. My tree is in the middle and they are all connected with swirls. The mark moves gently, like it's alive.

"What does it look like?" she asks me. My lips part with no words as I run my hand over the marks, feeling the slight power from each of them. We are finally all together, like it's always meant to be.

"Complete," I say and I lean down to kiss her. I spend the night with my queen and "complete" is the only word to describe it.

CHAPTER 28

"*Winter, my baby girl,*" *I open my eyes to a frozen field, there's a large willow tree on top of the hill, its long branches blowing in the cold wind. Elissa is standing next to a woman I know, but it's still a big shock.*

My mother stands in front of me, in the same white dress as Elissa. Her long, brown hair sways in the cold wind like Elissa's black hair does. When they are next to each other, I can see the similarities. They look so alike, but my mother's gaze is filled with love and tears. I want to run to her, but I can't. My heart pounds against my chest as I meet her blue eyes, just like mine.

"*It's not safe, and he'll do what he did to me. You need to wake up and run,*" *she pleads with me, her words desperate.*

"You're dead?" I ask, and she nods. I knew it, but I had to hear it.

"Yes, many years ago, when my father called me to him. My father can call his own blood, it's like your dream-calling power, but he can control you. He didn't expect his demons to want to feed on me when he sent them to take me through a portal. They did and killed me, but that was a blessing because he couldn't find you. My father has to be close to you for him to have control, you have to run," she says. The wind blows snow against my cheeks, and I blink the cold away as I focus on her words.

She steps close to me.

"How can I call the dead?" I ask.

"Because our spirits never left you. I will never leave you, my child. War is coming, and your heart will break, I only wish I could hold you as it does," she says, making me worry; her words can't be true. I refuse to believe them.

I realise she can't touch me when she hovers her impossibly pale hand over my shoulder; we are exactly the same height as she stands so close to me.

"I dream-called your friend, Lily, she is going to help me win the war," I say, looking over every detail of her face. How she has freckles, but I don't. How her nose is slightly different from mine, but we have the same lips.

"She is no friend; that was a grave mistake, Winter. The

price is too high for the promise," she tells me, and I feel sick. What have I done?

"I don't—" I say, and my mother cuts me off.

"You can fight him; your mates can save you."

"Only her mates can stop her from the destruction of all," Elissa says as she moves next to my mother. Her bright blue eyes meet mine.

"Remember that, remember the words," Elissa says, and the sky turns black slowly as I turn my head to watch. The cold air becomes painful to breathe in as my mother and Elissa disappear. I can't see their faces as the cold wind pushes me over into the snow. I stand up shakily and watch as the demon king walks over the hill.

"Thank you for accepting my call," he says and laughs.

I wake up and jump in the bed, nearly falling off the side.

I glance at the empty bed, and I wonder where Atti is. A shaking fills the castle, and the bed slides on the floor. The window blasts open near the bed. I scream and pull the sheets closer around myself.

What's happening?

I didn't expect to wake up from finally mating with Atti to this. I blush when I think of the night with Atti, but the shaking castle soon snaps me back to reality.

I need to find Atti and tell him about the dream; I need to make sure he's alright. I get up in the dark bedroom and pull Atti's shirt off the floor and over my head, it hits my knees with how large it is. The castle shakes again, and I fall to the ground. I think a witch or several must be using their earth powers. It's not Jaxson, he went back to the pack with Wyatt after the fight.

The door is slammed open, and I scramble back as the demon king walks in. He smirks down at me, a look of pure evil on his pale face. The demon king's face is covered in blue veins, but they are nothing on his glowing, dark-red eyes. They're nothing like mine when they glow; no, they are scary. The demon king has a long, black cloak over his clothes and the vampire crown on his head. He looks so much like Wyatt's father, but everything is harder and lost because of the demon controlling his body.

"Time to come with me, my princess," he says and holds out a hand. I hold my throat as something takes over me. I can't move, and I fall to my knees as pain takes over my body in a wave.

Suddenly, I feel nothing.

My mind screams "no" as my body ignores me and stands up. I walk over to the demon king and place my hand in his with a large smile spreading over my face. *Why am I smiling?*

The demon king leads me over to an older witch with long, black hair. The dark witch bows, and looks at the demon king with clear desire. I try to scream in my head, I try to move my body as I feel darkness slipping over my mind.

"Time to destroy the world, my princess," the demon king laughs. I don't refuse him as the witch takes us away, and darkness turns everything black.

R ead the next book by clicking here…

AUTHOR NOTE

Hello, and thank you for reading Winter's Promise!
A review would be amazing, and I would love you
for it.
Thank you to all my amazing fans for their support.
Most of all I want to say thank you to everyone that
bought this book, you guys and gals are amazing!
A special shout out to Anna and Taylor, my
awesome betas. Also a thank you to Michelle and
Meagan!

BONUS READ

I knew nothing about mates until the alpha rejected me...

Growing up in one of the biggest packs in the world, I have my life planned out for me from the second I turn eighteen and find my true mate in the moon ceremony.

Finding your true mate gives you the power to share the shifter energy they have, given to the males of the pack by the moon goddess herself. The power to shift into a wolf.

But for the first time in the history of our pack, the new alpha is mated with a nobody. A foster kid living in the pack's orphanage with no ancestors or power to claim.

Me.

After being brutally rejected by my alpha mate,
publicly humiliated and thrown away into the sea,
the dark wolves of the Fall Mountain Pack find me.
They save me. The four alphas. The ones the world
fears because of the darkness they live in.
In their world? Being rejected is the only way to join
their pack. The only way their lost and forbidden
god gives them the power to shift without a mate.

I spent my life worshipping the moon goddess,
when it turns out my life always belonged to
another...

*This is a full-length reverse harem romance novel full of sexy
alpha males, steamy scenes, a strong heroine and a lot of
sarcasm. Intended for 17+ readers. This is a trilogy.*

*C*hapter One:
            "Don't hide from us, little pup. Don't
you want to play with the wolves?"

Beta Valeriu's voice rings out around me as I
duck under the staircase of the empty house,
dodging a few cobwebs that get trapped in my long
blonde hair. Breathlessly, I sink to the floor and
wrap my arms around my legs, trying not to
breathe in the thick scent of damp and dust.

Closing my eyes, I pray to the moon goddess that they will get bored with chasing me, but I know better. No goddess is going to save my ass tonight. Not when I'm being hunted by literal wolves.

I made a mistake. A big mistake. I went to a party in the pack, like all my other classmates at the beta's house, to celebrate the end of our schooling and, personally for me, turning eighteen. For some tiny reason, I thought I could be normal for one night. Be like them.

And not just one of the foster kids the pack keeps alive because of the laws put in place by a goddess no one has seen in hundreds of years. I should have known the betas in training would get drunk and decide chasing me for another one of their "fun" beatings would be a good way to prove themselves.

Wiping the blood from my bottom lip where one of them caught me in the forest with his fist, I stare at my blood-tipped fingers in a beam of moonlight shining through the broken panelled wall behind me.

I don't know why I think anyone is going to save me. I'm nothing to them, the pack, or to the moon goddess I pray to every night like everyone in this pack does.

The moon goddess hasn't saved me from shit.

Heavy footsteps echo closer, changing from crunching leaves to hitting concrete floor, and I know they are in the house now. A rat runs past my leg, and I nearly scream as I jolt backwards into a loose metal panel that vibrates, the metal smacking against another piece and revealing my location to the wolves hunting me.

Crap.

My hands shake as I climb to my feet and slowly step out into the middle of the room as Beta Valeriu comes in with his two sidekicks, who stumble to his side. I glance around the room, seeing the staircase is broken and there is an enormous gap on the second floor. It looks burnt out from a fire, but there is no other exit. I'm well and truly in trouble now. They stop in an intimidating line, all three of them muscular and jacked up enough to knock a car over. Their black hair is all the same shade, likely because they are all cousins, I'm sure, and they have deeply tanned skin that doesn't match how pale my skin is. Considering I'm a foster kid, I could have at least gotten the same looks as them, but oh no, the moon goddess gave me bright blonde hair that never stops growing fast and freckly pale skin to stand out. I look like the

G. BAILEY

moon comparing itself to the beauty of the sun
with everyone in my pack.

Beta Valeriu takes a long sip of his drink, his
eyes flashing green, his wolf making it clear he
likes the hunt. Valeriu is the newest beta, taking
over from his father, who recently retired at two
hundred years of age and gave the role to his son
willingly. But Valeriu is a dick. Simple as. He
might be good-looking, like most of the five betas
are, but each one of them lacks a certain amount
of brain cells. The thing is, wolves don't need to
be smart to be betas, they just need the right
bloodline and to kill when the alpha clicks his
fingers.

All wolves like to hunt and kill. And damn, I'm
always the hunted in this pack.

"You know better than to run from us, little
Mairin. Little Mary the lamb who runs from the
wolf," he sing songs the last part, taking a slow step
forward, his shoe grating across the dirt under his
feet. Always the height jokes with this tool. He
might be over six foot, and sure, my five foot three
height isn't intimidating, but has no one heard the
phrase *small but deadly*?

Even if I'm not even a little deadly. "Who
invited you to my party?"

"The entire class in our pack was invited," I bite out.

He laughs, the crisp sound echoing around me like a wave of frost. "We both know you might be in this pack, but that's only because of the law about killing female children. Otherwise, our alpha would have ripped you apart a long time ago."

Yeah, I know the law. The law that states female children cannot be killed because of the lack of female wolves born into the pack. There is roughly one female to five wolves in the pack, and it's been that way for a long time for who knows what reason. So, when they found me in the forest at twelve, with no memories and nearly dead, they had to take me in and save my life.

A life, they have reminded me daily, has only been given to me because of that law. The law doesn't stop the alpha from treating me like crap under his shoe or beating me close to death for shits and giggles. Only me, though. The other foster kid I live with is male, so he doesn't get the "special" attention I do. Thankfully.

"We both know you can't kill me or beat me bad enough to attract attention without the alpha here. So why don't you just walk away and find some poor dumbass girl to keep you busy at the party?" I blurt out, tired of all this. Tired of never saying what I want to these idiots and fearing the alpha all the time. A bitter laugh escapes Valeriu's mouth as his eyes fully glow this time. So do his friends', as I realise I just crossed a line with my smart-ass mouth.

My foster carer always said my mouth would get me into trouble.

Seems he is right once again.

A threatening growl explodes from Beta Valeriu's chest, making all the hairs on my arms stand up as I take a step back just as he shifts. I've seen it a million times, but it's always amazing and terrifying at the same time. Shifter energy, pure dark forest green magic, explodes around his body as he changes shape. The only sound in the room is his clicking bones and my heavy, panicked breathing as I search for a way out of here once again, even though I know it's pointless.

I've just wound up a wolf. A beta wolf, one of the most powerful in our pack.

Great job, Irin. Way to stay alive.

The shifter magic disappears, leaving a big white wolf in the space where Valeriu was. The wolf towers over me, like most of them do, and its head is huge enough to eat me with one bite. Just as he steps forward to jump, and I brace myself for something painful, a shadow of a man jumps down from the broken slats above me, landing with a thump. Dressed in a white cloak over jeans and a shirt, my foster carer completely blocks me from Valeriu's view, and I sigh in relief.

"I suggest you leave before I teach you what an experienced, albeit retired, beta wolf can do to a young pup like yourself. Trust me, it will hurt, and our alpha will look the other way."

The threat hangs in the air, spoken with an authority that Valeriu could never dream of having in his voice at eighteen years old. The room goes silent, filled with thick tension for a long time before I hear the wolf running off, followed by two pairs of footsteps moving quickly. My badass foster carer slowly turns around, lowering his hood and brushing his long grey hair back from his face. Smothered in wrinkles, Mike is ancient, and to this day, I have no clue why he offered to work with the foster kids of the pack. His blue eyes remind me of the pale sea I saw once when I was twelve. He always dresses like a Jedi from the human movies, in long cloaks and swords clipped to his hips that look like lightsabres as they glow with magic, and he tells me this is his personal style.

His name is even more human than most of the pack names that get regularly overused. My name, which is the only thing I know about my past thanks to a note in my hand, is as uncommon as it gets. According to an old book on names, it means Their Rebellion, which makes no sense. Mike is apparently a normal human name, and from the little interaction I've had with humans through their technology, his name couldn't be more common.

"You are extremely lucky my back was playing up and I went for a walk, Irin," he sternly comments, and I sigh.

"I'm sorry," I reply, knowing there isn't much else I can say at this point. "The mating ceremony is tomorrow, and I wanted one night of being normal. I shouldn't have snuck out of the foster house."

"No, you should not have when your freedom is so close," he counters and reaches up, gently pinching my chin with his fingers and turning my head to the side. "Your lip is cut, and there is considerable bruising to your cheek. Do you like being beaten by those pups?"

"No, of course not," I say, tugging my face away, still tasting my blood in my mouth. "I wanted to be normal! Why is that so much to ask?"

"Normal is for humans and not shifters. It is why they gave us the United Kingdom and Ireland and then made walls around the islands to stop us from getting out. They want normal, and we need nothing more than what is here: our pack," he begins, telling me what I already know. They agreed three hundred years ago we would take this part of earth as our own, and the humans had the rest. No one wanted interbreeding, and this was the best way to keep peace. So the United Kingdom's lands were separated into four packs. One in England, one in Wales, one in Scotland and one in Ireland. Now there are just two packs, thanks to the shifter wars: the Ravensword Pack that is my home, who worship the moon goddess, and then the Fall Mountain Pack, who owns Ireland, a pack we are always at war with. Whoever they worship, it isn't our goddess, and everything I know about them suggests they are brutal. Unfeeling. Cruel.

Which is exactly why I've never tried to leave my pack to go there. It might be shit here, but at least it's kind of safe and I have a future. Of sorts.

"Do you think it will be better for me when I find my mate tomorrow?" I question…not that I want a mate who will control me with his shifter energy. But it means I will shift into a wolf, like every female can when they are mated, and I've always wanted that.

Plus, a tiny part of me wants to know who the moon goddess herself has chosen for me. The other half of my soul. My true mate. Someone who won't see me as the foster kid who has no family, and will just want me.

Mike looks down at me, and something unreadable crosses his eyes. He turns away and starts walking out of the abandoned house, and I jog to catch up with him. Snowflakes drop into my blonde hair as we head through the forest, back to the foster home, the place I will finally leave one way or another tomorrow. I pull my leather jacket around my chest, over my brown T-shirt for warmth. My torn and worn out jeans are soaked with snow after a few minutes of walking, the snow becoming thicker with every minute. Mike is silent as we walk past the rocks that mark the small pathway until we get to the top of the hill that overlooks the main pack city of Ravensword.

Towering buildings line the River Thames that flows through the middle of the city. The bright lights make it look like a reflection of the stars in the sky, and the sight is beautiful. It might be a messed up place, but I can't help but admire it. I remember the first time I saw the city from here, a few days after I was found and healed. I remember thinking I had woken up from hell to see heaven, but soon I learnt heaven was too nice of a word for this place. The night is silent up here, missing the usual noise of the people in the city, and I silently stare down wondering why we have stopped.

"What do you see when you look at the city, Irin?"

I blow out a long breath. "Somewhere I need to escape."

I don't see his disappointment, but I easily feel it.

"I see my home, a place with darkness in its corners but so much light. I see a place even a foster wolf with no family or ancestors to call on can find happiness tomorrow," he responds. "Stop looking at the stars for your escape, Irin, because tomorrow you will find your home in the city you are trying so hard to see nothing but darkness in."

He carries on walking, and I follow behind him, trying to do what he has asked, but within seconds my eyes drift up to the stars once again.

Because Mike is right, I am always looking for my way to escape, and I always will. I wasn't born in this pack, and I came from outside the walls that have been up for hundreds of years. That's the only explanation for how they found me in a forest with nothing more than a small glass bottle in my hand and a note with my name on it. No one knows how that is possible, least of all me, but somehow I'm going to figure it out. I have to.

Read the next book by clicking here...